THE
BOOK
OF
SAM

ROB SHAPIRO

THE
BOOK
OF
SAM

DUNDURN
TORONTO

Publisher: Scott Fraser | Acquiring editor: Rachel Spence | Editor: Susan Fitzgerald
Cover desiger: Sophie Paas-Lang
Cover image: istock.com/JoZtar

Library and Archives Canada Cataloguing in Publication

Title: The book of Sam / Rob Shapiro.
Names: Shapiro, Rob, 1982- author.
Identifiers: Canadiana (print) 20190213566 | Canadiana (ebook) 20190213574 | ISBN 9781459746756 (softcover) | ISBN 9781459746763 (PDF) | ISBN 9781459746770 (EPUB)
Classification: LCC PS8637.H3648 B66 2020 | DDC jC813/.6—dc23

We acknowledge the support of the Canada Council for the Arts and the Ontario Arts Council for our publishing program. We also acknowledge the financial support of the Government of Ontario, through the Ontario Book Publishing Tax Credit and Ontario Creates, and the Government of Canada.

VISIT US AT

dundurn.com | @dundurnpress | dundurnpress | dundurnpress

Dundurn
3 Church Street, Suite 500
Toronto, Ontario, Canada
M5E 1M2

For Natalie

HARPER JAMES

Where is she? I thought as I sat on the steps of my front porch, a safe distance from the noise of my family. Inside my house a PlayStation controller pounded amid video game gunfire, heavy feet ran up and down the stairs, and above all that, my dad screamed at my mom about something I did or left on or forgot to put away or whatever. I didn't pay much attention to it, lost in my own head.

Harper was almost an hour late. The plan was to go to Queens Quay to board a ferry to the Islands. There, we'd spend a night huddled around a bonfire on Ward's Island. I'd been looking forward to this night all week, the first that Harper didn't have family stuff or cheerleading practice or a model UN meeting.

I leaned back, my elbows pressed against the wood, trying to see around the house on the corner, hoping Harper would pop into view.

I hadn't seen her since Justin Breslow's party the Friday before. His parents were in Las Vegas, so he'd announced to the cafeteria that there would be a party at his house. Since I was at the back of the room, I was officially invited, even if I was eating alone. So I went — and by *went*, I mean I stood in a corner, talking to Harper as she fended off guys trying to press up against her. I walked her home, and before we parted I asked her if we could hang out on the Islands next week, one of her last before she was going to leave for Paris on an academic exchange. I had applied for the same program, but was told that my application didn't meet their standards. She happily agreed to my proposal before kissing my cheek.

I checked my phone for the hundredth time. No texts, but a couple dozen Snapchat notifications, which I was sure were about some party I wasn't invited to. I made a mental note to check later.

That annoying voice in my head started yapping, conjuring scenarios where something bad had happened. Harper lived only a block away and had walked the short distance to my house thousands of times without a problem. Both of our streets touched what was once Toronto's boardwalk, the Esplanade. It's a ribbon of road that runs east to west along shimmering Lake Ontario, and it once buzzed with the noise of distilleries, refineries, twirling carousels, and transport trains rushing into stations. Eventually, the trains were moved above and below ground, the carousels were dismantled — the sad painted horses packed into kitschy restaurants to amuse kids as their parents ate — and the distilleries and refineries were shut down to make way for new industries. Toronto expanded south. Like prison bars, condo buildings cut the city off from the water, though I still liked to tell people that I lived by the lake. It was more interesting than saying I lived near the new forty-five-storey condo on top of a Whole Foods.

Whatever action was happening on the Esplanade was not spilling onto my street, where the only things going on were a dog peeing on a flowerbed, some discarded flyers cartwheeling across the pavement, and Jake Springer, a kid from my school, helping his dad change the oil in their car. His dad wiped the dipstick with a grey cloth, plunged it into the oil tank, and pulled it out, teaching Jake to read the level.

The shouting from inside my house grew harsher. I walked to the window and snuck a look through a gap in the curtains. My sister Amy marched down the stairs and passed like a ship through choppy waters between my parents arguing in the hallway. She was the oldest of the kids and the most immune to the stress of our home. I couldn't make out what my parents were saying, but I heard my name. I'd done something wrong.

I retreated to the steps of the porch, but this time I chose the bottom one to give myself a little more distance. I tapped my feet to the beat of the song I was humming, trying to think happy thoughts: bunny rabbits, baseball, Harper — that kind of stuff.

Finally, Harper appeared from around the corner, her face blocked by a bubble of pink gum. The sight of her quieted the noise from my family as if a steel door had hermetically sealed them off. Her hands were shoved into the pockets of her ripped jeans, and her brown hair was pulled into a ponytail except for two strands that bracketed her face. She threw me a half-hearted wave and a practised smile, which wilted in seconds. Harper was as subtle as a marching band, and even from a distance, her mood was evident. Something was wrong.

We met at the bottom of the steps for a hug — a big warm one without any restraint, her arms squeezing around my neck. How many more hugs did we have before she left?

"Ready to go?" I said.

She tilted her head down and stared at her shoes, kicking the toe of one against the ground. Her nose crinkled as if she smelled something pungent.

"I don't wanna go anymore," she said, her voice barbed.

"Why not? We've been planning this all week." I was annoyed.

"I'm just not in the mood anymore," she said. She breathed in and her eyes looked upwards at the clouds to avoid contact with mine. I was starting to think her hug had been a pity hug, a sorry-your-aunt-didn't-make-it hug. She crossed her arms.

"Have you looked at your snaps in the last hour?" she said, not quite managing to sound casual.

I shook my head. "No, but my phone's been blowing up. Why?"

She adjusted her ponytail even though it was fine. She crossed her arms again and then uncrossed them.

"What is it?" I said. "You're being weird."

"Maybe we should go inside," Harper said.

She took my hand and pulled me up the porch steps. I tensed, wondering what she was going to show me. Did someone post something about her? A pic no one was supposed to see? That had happened to a girl we knew, Priya. She was a quiet girl who'd met a guy online. After some pleading and manipulating on his part, she sent him a topless selfie. The next day it was on the screen of every phone and tablet at school, a cruel prank by a popular girl, who told the principal she did it out of boredom.

My house was a zoo. My youngest brother, Stephen, was swearing under his breath as he played a video game in the living room, his feet propped on the coffee table in front of an opened bag of chips. Amy was running back and forth between her bedroom and the laundry room, dropping a trail of socks and tank tops from the mound of clothes she was carrying. My other brother, Aaron, was in the backyard hitting whiffle balls against the house. Only my other sister, Bethany, the quiet intellectual, was still. She sat at the dining room table with a textbook cracked open, taking notes on her tablet. If you think being a middle child is tough, try being one of three.

I much preferred hanging out at Harper's house. Her family was kind and quiet. They giggled and ate breakfast together. Her parents would always lift their heads from a book or mute a television show to say goodnight to their kids. My dad, on the other hand, liked to give me daily reminders that I was sixteen years old and needed to stop acting like a child.

I slammed the front door to alert my parents that we had a guest. They stopped shouting as soon as they saw Harper. My mom, wearing her usual look of frustration, was petite, with short brown hair and freckles.

She looked exhausted, evidenced by the light-purple bags under her eyes. She wasn't yet fifty but looked like she'd experienced a century's worth of fried nerves. My dad was silent, looking through me as he always did. His black hair was thinning, his temples salted white. His gut sloped over his belt, and he pulled his broad shoulders back before letting out a deep, annoyed breath.

My mom gave me a look. *Go upstairs.*

Harper and I went into my bedroom and closed the door. I flopped onto my twin bed, knocking an empty ramen container off the messy blanket. Harper sat next to me, thumbing the screen of her phone, which she'd angled away to shield from my view.

"Seriously, what's going on? Are we really not going?"

No reply. Harper could have been a million miles away in that moment. She was rarely this quiet. She was more the type to stand up in a crowded movie theatre and scream at the idiot character for running upstairs to escape the killer. Every movement of her thumb filled me with worry. I steeled myself against whatever I was about to learn.

"Okay," she said.

She turned the phone to face me. As soon as I saw what was on the screen, I felt as if an airlock had opened, letting all the air in the room escape in a loud whoosh. A black-and-white pic of me sitting alone in the cafeteria, the word *Monday* written at the bottom. This was followed by a series of similar photos, one for each weekday. Every pic was a portrait of me looking sad and sullen, surrounded by but separated from students frozen in a state of natural happiness. Harper clicked to another pic. This one showed me sitting alone on a grassy island in the quad. As I looked at the pics, sweat pooled on my palms and in my armpits. My face didn't just become hot; it was on fire. A whole album cataloguing my loneliness existed online and would exist online forever. Below the first pic was a lengthening thread of comments: "fag," "loser," "LAME AF," "kill yourself, Sam — signed everyone," "No one would miss that guy," "basic," "who dis?"

My chest seemed to cave in when I saw the last photo. I immediately recognized the locker room. In front of my open locker I stood completely naked, reaching to hang a towel on the inside hook, my pasty backside exposed in all its glory. The patches of hair on my shoulders, the red constellation of back acne — it was all there.

I went limp, and tears stung my eyes. Harper fell onto her back, her hands on her head.

"That's why I was late. I was trying to fix this," she said.

I stared at the background photo on my laptop: a pic of me and Harper biting into cronuts at the Canadian National Exhibition last summer. I couldn't bear looking at her. I just wanted to die.

"Say something," Harper said.

"Who did this?" I whispered, unable to find my voice.

"That asshole Kyle. He got the pics from his friends on the yearbook committee."

"Why was the yearbook staff in the locker room?"

Harper sat up. "I don't know, but we're gonna tell your parents, the school, the police, everyone — I don't care."

An image of Kyle McGee formed in my mind: his moon face, patchy moustache, and bushy eyebrows. The only thing he loved more than his fauxhawk was calling me a fag, a freak, and a retard, which he had done consistently since grade six. He took pleasure in embarrassing me and making sure I was always aware of my shortcomings, which included being bad at sports, math, and music; being uncoordinated; having acne; getting banned from the AV club; and generally failing at most things. Over the years, he had whipped snowballs at my head, pulled my pants to my ankles as I walked down the hall, punched me while I stood defenceless at a urinal, and spat in my food. Now that we were older, his taunts had matured and become crueller. He had gotten the whole school to laugh at me.

Dread hung in the air of my room, thick as fog. We sat at the edge of my bed, our eyes fixed on the wall. Harper leaned forward, her elbows on her knees, her gum cracking in her mouth. If she were a cartoon character, steam would have been blowing out of her ears.

To say she was protective of me was an understatement. We had a running joke about how many days I would survive without her. She bet on five, but the smart money was on three. Even my family got in on the fun.

My greatest fear was about to be realized. In two weeks, there would be an ocean between us. She would be in another corner of the world, learning and having the experience of a lifetime. She would make new friends and meet exotic boys in berets, and I could already imagine how the number of emails would dwindle week by week until our relationship withered to just being old friends.

"I'm gonna kill him," she said, not breaking her stare. I'd always been an anxious guy, and the thought of that comment thread growing through the night and over the next day and the day after made my stomach hurt. A thought I'd had for years nagged me: nothing would ever change except to get worse.

"Snaps expire, at least," I said.

"They're also on Instagram and Facebook, and someone hacked the school's homepage."

A tear rolled out of the corner of my eye. I wiped it away. "Maybe people will forget about this in a few days."

"You say that every time and they never just forget," she said, her voice shaded with disappointment. "They always find new ways to bully you."

Harper inched over and placed her hand on my back. Our watery eyes and flushed cheeks reminded me of when we were kids and she'd console me over a playground beating. I looked at the floor where we used to roll out sleeping bags and lay on top of them, swirling our flashlights on the ceiling until my dad yelled at us to go to bed. Life was simpler then.

"I have to go," I said, not wanting to be the subject of her pity.

"Sam, you can't just run away. You need to deal with this," she said. "Stop being such a … a …"

Instead of finishing her sentence, she dropped her arms in defeat. She seemed to be feeling a rising tide of anger, as I was, but as usual, we handled our emotions differently. My brain started to throb. I rubbed my forehead, trying to alleviate the pressure building behind my eyebrows.

"You have to stand up for yourself. You have to do something for once and not just hide," she said, her emotion bubbling to the surface.

We were deathly quiet. I had no idea how to defuse the situation. She took my hand and held it tightly.

"I'm sorry," she said softly.

I needed to be alone. Despite her pleading, I left Harper in my room and headed to Dundas Street to catch a streetcar west.

2
CLOAKED ATLAS

A twilight version of the city slowly slid by the streetcar windows. As we approached a busy intersection, I pulled the cord and got out at the corner of Dundas and Spadina Avenue, the heart of Chinatown.

Everywhere was crowded: the sidewalks, crosswalks, and bus shelters. People spilled out of restaurants and bars. Escape was impossible. My mood was lodged in some sort of abyss as I walked under the streetlamps activated by the night, past an old Chinese bakery, some trendy coffee shops, and a small fruit market. I arrived at a frosted-glass door nestled between the oldest dim sum restaurant in Toronto and a comic book shop. Above the door hung a sign:

CLOAKED ATLAS
BOOKS / MAPS / ARTIFACTS

I'm not much of an adventurer — big spoiler, right? My uncle, on the other hand, is a full-blown, no-holds-barred, grab-the-bull-by-the-horns, sword-between-his-teeth adventurer. His life's work can be found in a dusty shop on the second floor of an old building in Chinatown.

Since it was after business hours, I had to unlock the street door. The staircase that led to my uncle's shop was awash in the red glow of an overhead emergency light. I ran up the steps, and with one more turn of a key I was inside, cut off from the world. I was safe.

Moonlight bathed the cigar-scented interior appointed in dark walnut. The silvery light allowed me glimpses of the slowly rotating ceiling fan and the elevator that my uncle had built for accessibility. Bookcases filled with leather-bound books dominated the walls. Between two bookcases was a cozy reading nook with a circular rug, a purple wingback chair, and small end table. At the back was a glass jewellery case that needed a good cleaning. Swords hung close to the ceiling, spaced evenly across the wall. As a kid, I used to climb up the shelving to reach a sword, only to have my uncle grab me and place me back on the floor. It wasn't until I was ten that he let me hold one.

Cloaked Atlas opened its doors in 1995, yet after a couple of decades, most Torontonians still didn't know it existed. The more the city became engulfed by high-rises and chains, the more the nondescript shop seemed to fade from public view and float above street level in some alternate world. It wasn't a place for idle shopping. The only time I remember it getting foot traffic was during the Pokémon GO craze, but all those people left the shop Pikachu-less, some even crying after being yelled at by an old man who didn't appreciate trends in mobile gaming.

The shop was home to the unique items and artifacts that Uncle Bear obsessed over. He had turned a Ph.D. in archeology into a life of globetrotting adventure. His stories were the stuff of legend: treasure hunts through foggy London nights, uprisings in the streets of Giza, meetings with shadowy figures in the secret rooms of St. Peter's Basilica. It was only after a dangerous excursion to Jakarta that he was forced to settle down. As he tells it, he was being chased across a rooftop when he tried to leap between buildings. Despite his best efforts, which were usually good enough, he missed the mark and fell through a series of awnings, landing on a spice stand in a crowded market. The result was a broken vertebra, the rest of his life in a wheelchair, and smelling like cumin for a week. Uncle Bear was never one to focus on the negative. He came home to Toronto and created a mecca for dealers, traders, and merchants from all over the world. He always said that if he hadn't broken his back, he never would have met Raymond, his partner. Raymond had always been kind to me. In my next life, I hoped I would get them as parents.

Uncle Bear did *not* collect antiques. In fact, he would stab anyone who called his treasures antiques with a gladius that had been used by an actual Roman foot soldier. He reserved that derogatory term for dainty Russian statues and Fabergé eggs — the scourge of the industry, as he called them.

I worked at Cloaked Atlas a few nights a week, giving my uncle and Raymond some nights off to go to the movies. Besides Harper, Uncle Bear was the person I was closest to and the shop was my true home. In the shop, there were no tests bludgeoned by a red pen or team rosters minus my name. There were no meetings with the guidance counsellor, Mr. Clapp, who liked to remind me that repeating the eleventh grade was always an option. There was no Kyle or fear that any passing snicker or whispered word was secretly directed at me.

It was because of my uncle that I didn't believe in monsters. He made me stand in front of a mirror and say "Bloody Mary" three times to prove that it didn't make a monster appear in order to feast on me. It was my uncle who had me reclaim my closet from nightmarish intruders. He once found me under my bed and when he asked what monster had driven me there, I simply replied that kids at school didn't want to play with me.

I had a small bedroom in the back of the shop. When I stayed there, I had to follow my uncle's strict rules: up before the cry of seven, bed impeccably made before I left the room, shop cleaned before breakfast, and I had to keep my bicycle hanging from hooks in the storage room. For a man who had lived such a wild life, he really enjoyed a nicely made bed.

My uncle and I had always been close, but our relationship had taken off a few years before, after an incident at a family dinner. My entire family was there, celebrating Aaron's being named MVP of the Greater Toronto Hockey League. After several toasts and speeches in my brother's honour, my dad stood up and told us how proud he was of Aaron, the hockey star, and Bethany, the honours student. He gushed about Stephen, who was the youngest student at his prestigious arts school, and got a little choked up when he congratulated Amy on her acceptance to law school. He then looked at me and announced to the table that some young men just mature late.

Uncle Bear turned to me and reassured me that the true greats don't need acclaim or validation, and that in his heart, he knew I was destined for big things. I saw him yelling at my dad outside the restaurant before he rode off in a cab. After that night, I spent a lot more time at Cloaked Atlas. It was there that I read books that weren't offered in school. They taught me new words and expressions and gave me an appreciation of some of life's finer things and an understanding of how big the world was. Of course, none of this made me more popular. If anything, it created more distance between me and the other kids. I sat on the floor, hugging my knees and thinking about the future. In two weeks, Harper would be gone and I'd be even more alone. I let my face fall into my hands, my breathing now a childish whimper.

As I wiped my eyes with my sleeve, I noticed the corner of a book poking out from underneath a bookcase, the initials *M.W.F.R.* just visible in faint cursive. As if it were calling to me, I pulled out the coverless book and wiped away a layer of dust with my hand. The words on the first page felt familiar. My uncle used to read me this book. It was about a demon named Stolas who rose from the life of a slave to rule Hell. Not the boring Hell people learn about in church. My uncle was in no way religious. Actually, religion was the only thing he and my dad agreed on. These were stories of demons, creatures, sorcerers, and an emperor. I remembered my uncle telling me that these stories were very old and that he had learned about them in his travels. It was mythology pretending to be history, and I loved every word on every page. But I guess I eventually outgrew them.

I started reading, and instantly I was seven years old again, swept away by Stolas's life: a demon destined to die a slave, but he refused and instead waged a war to make sure others never suffered the same fate. He fought in great battles, moved crowds with his words, and worked to create a better, fairer world. He defeated the vicious Emperor Belphegor in a fortressed city that the emperor had constructed at the centre of Hell and named after himself. For his sacrifice, Stolas was dubbed the Liberator of Belphegor.

At some point, the sun broke through the curtains. I was only a few pages from the end when my eyelids became heavy. I succumbed to sleep, sprawled on the floor. My last thought was of Stolas standing atop the bell tower in his hometown of Ragewick, looking out over the land that he had rebuilt.

"Sam," an ashy voice said. "Sam."

A few drops of cold water landed on my face.

"Sam!"

I opened my eyes a crack to find Uncle Bear tipping a glass of water over my head, a knowing smile plastered on his face.

"Why are you pouring water on me?" I said as I wiped my face with the inside of my arm.

"I couldn't find my poking stick." He wheeled his chair back, giving me some room to sit up. "Why aren't you sleeping in your bed? Better yet, why aren't you at school? It's ten in the morning."

I sat up, my puffy eyes still adjusting to the sunlight. The shop always looked so different in the light of day. Uncle Bear wheeled himself over to the counter, where he collected a stack of receipts.

My uncle had aged so much in the last few years. His face was jowly and his chin hung down like a chicken's. His waist had expanded, and I hadn't seen his legs in years because he always kept them covered in this puke-green blanket. Spots on his scalp made it look like a game of battleship. Even his wheelchair squeaked more than it used to.

A kettle squealed. He disappeared into his office and returned a minute later carrying a steaming cup of tea with one hand, his other one manoeuvring his wheelchair.

"Remember this?" I said, holding up the book so that Uncle Bear could read the title on the spine.

"Of course, *The Book of Stolas*, a classic. I haven't seen it in some time," he said. "You used to love those stories. Stolas and Emperor Belphegor and the Architects of Hell." He gave me a nostalgic smile. "So what is it, Sam, trouble at home?"

"It's everything — Harper, my dad, school." I got up and stretched my arms and back. I didn't want to tell him about Kyle or Snapchat because I knew it would just be an invitation for a colourful anecdote about revenge — and then he'd ask me what Snapchat was.

"Harper is not a problem. Most don't even get one Harper in their entire lives, so count your blessings. And I hate to speak ill of your father." He paused, seeming to think. "But he's a total schmuck. Why Pat married him is a mystery for the ages."

Pat was my mom. You would never know it from her perfect book-club attendance or the way she was always running around the house yelling, but she was once a world-travelling surfer, a carefree version of her much older and more serious brother. On a trip to Tofino she met a law student named Glen who was there on a frat trip. He was watching the sunset from the roof of his car. Within a year, she had hung up the surfboard, gotten married, and settled into a basement apartment in Corktown. My uncle and mom used to have big dreams, and he always resented the fact that she quit on them so young. He often reminded me that he loved all his nieces and nephews, but that I was the best gift his sister had ever given him.

"Well, my boy, if you're going to be a truant, then let's do it right. Two swords."

I pulled down our usual two swords and handed him one. I took the starting position that he had taught me, and we began to spar. He barely looked at me as he blocked every one of my strikes. After a minute, I was exhausted and he was done his tea.

"You've gotten much better over the years, but you need to focus on that one decisive strike," he said. "Now, follow me."

I followed him past the standing globe, jewellery case, and cash register into his office. Everything in the room was tinged yellow from cigar smoke, and the mahogany desk was covered in papers and receipts. A vintage Texas Instruments calculator rested on top of a map of Prussia. His computer took the cake, though — he'd had me remove the keys he thought were pointless, giving it a jack-o'-lantern smile.

He picked up a pad of paper and a pencil from beside his computer and started jotting something down. I pulled a chair from the corner and sat across from him.

"Is this about Paris?" Uncle Bear said, not lifting his eyes from the pad of paper.

"I don't know what to do," I said. "I've had most of my life to tell her about … ya know, my feelings and stuff, but I never had the guts to."

"C'mon, Sam, take a chance for once," Uncle Bear said. He picked up a tattered cigar from the groove in an ashtray and placed it between his teeth. He didn't light it, opting to just suck on the end.

I leaned back, knowing his advice was good. But if it were that easy, I would have told Harper how I felt about her when I was twelve. Baring my feelings defied every instinct I had, but my uncle's advice was always on point. If he told you to buy one brand of flour instead of another, you could be sure that his flour would produce fluffier pastries.

Uncle Bear could read anyone. I loved to watch him haggle with salespeople who came into the shop, many of whom had travelled great distances to sell something to him specifically. He could sniff out a fraud the moment the bell over the door dinged. With just a glance, he would know if the salesperson's possession was prized, what its resale value was, and whether it was one of the few treasures that belonged in his own collection. One salesman, with a thick build, a flat head, and skin that looked like it had been badly dipped in bronzer, was so distraught from my uncle's rejection that he would appear on my walk from school to the shop every day for weeks. At first he would walk past me, tipping his hat hello. This evolved to stopping me for a quick chat about baseball and the weather. Finally, he would hold me by the elbow, threatening that if I didn't talk to Bear on his behalf, there would be consequences.

My uncle's private collection was kept secret from the world in a room connected to the office. The only way in was through a door that was blocked by a desk. That was all I knew, since I've never actually been inside. In fact, the only time my uncle ever scolded me was when I was eleven and he came into his office and saw the desk pulled out and my hand on the doorknob. I told him I just wanted to look around, but he made me place my right hand over my heart and promise that I would never go in there, that I would forget it even existed. Even the persuasive power of Harper could never convince me to stray from my pledge. Believe me, she'd tried.

Uncle Bear put down the pencil, ripped the sheet of paper from the pad, and handed it to me. I read aloud some of what he wrote, confused about what was going through his mind. "French baguette, beef broth, blue cheese, big bulb of garlic, one pound of PEI mussels, *House of Usher* (VHS)." The list was longer but I stopped reading and looked at my uncle, who was nodding along. "What is this?"

"No matter where I've travelled, no matter the year or the season or the people I've encountered, there has always been one unwaveringly universal truth," he said, holding a stern finger in the air.

I leaned forward, excited. "What? What is it?"

"Everyone, *and I mean everyone*, likes dinner and a movie."

"Huh?"

Uncle Bear threw me a wink. I looked at the list and realized it was a grocery list. The message was clear. I was going to make dinner for Harper and then we were going to watch the old Vincent Price movie, *House of Usher*. Fun fact about Harper: she was the world's biggest Vincent Price fan. One night we made guacamole using Vincent Price's recipe, which is an actual thing, and watched *Edward Scissorhands*. She hated the movie because Vincent Price was in only a few scenes.

"Not enough Vinnie P.," she would say whenever it came up.

Movies were the only thing we ever disagreed on, outside of how to deal with the Kyles of the world. Our biggest disagreement came after my mom made us watch *The Princess Bride*. I loved it. Harper not so much. She liked Fezzik but thought that Princess Buttercup was a useless damsel in distress.

"Ask Mrs. Choi downstairs if she can show you how to steam the mussels. She'll probably offer her kitchen. Raymond and I have plans tomorrow, so you can entertain Harper right here in the shop."

I smiled.

"Keep it simple, Sam, okay? A nice meal, good conversation, and tell her how you feel. Don't just let things happen. Make them happen."

He wheeled over and gave my cheek two quick, soft smacks with his hand. I replied with another smile.

"You're going to be okay, my boy," he said to me before leaving me alone in his office.

I stared at the list as if it were the magic elixir that would help me find the courage to finally do what I needed to do.

The next morning, I awoke to some folded cash that my uncle had left me on the night table and a text from Harper accepting my invitation for dinner and a movie. I was too scared to use the word *date*, but it didn't matter. Her reply had a couple more smiley emojis than usual.

I felt charged, the opposite of the day before, when my world was spinning out of control. I had a plan, and it definitely wasn't to show up at school and face hundreds of my peers who had gone from ignoring my existence to knowing exactly what my naked body looked like. I also wanted to avoid my family. I would have to stop at home to change at some point, sure, but sneaking in and out would be easy. The day was all mine to prepare for my "date."

I got dressed, took my bike down from its hooks, and, list in hand, rode east toward St. Lawrence Market, which looked like a massive firehouse but bustled with a carnival energy. Normally, preparing for something this big would have given me a fever and the shakes. For whatever reason, though, I was feeling light and a good, fluttering kind of anxious. Even so, my throat tightened at the thought of having to say the actual words while looking directly into Harper's big brown eyes.

I locked my bike to a post and headed through the thin crowd out front to join the thicker crowd that filled the old market. Under the high ceiling were butchers, fishmongers, and wine and cheese experts. The stalls were drenched in the aromas of roasting pork and fresh parsley and dill, with notes of salted fish and vinegar. Somehow it all came together to form one appetizing, familiar smell.

I checked the list one more time. Uncle Bear had kept it simple for me, knowing I wasn't going to succeed with a plan that required surgical execution.

My first stop was the seafood counter. A lab-coated worker scooped a pound of black mussels that still smelled like the Atlantic into a bag with some ice and wrapped the whole thing in butcher paper. Following the list, I bought a small hunk of blue cheese and then headed to the lower level for some garlic.

I left the market and pedalled toward my house. Five minutes later, I dropped my bike on my driveway and walked along the side of the house that led to our backyard. I hopped in the window well and crouched down. There was a broken latch on the window that my parents had never fixed, and we kids never reminded them because it gave us a nightly chance to escape. I pulled the window open and climbed inside.

I ran up the steps two at a time and down the hall-way. Dull music filled the upper floor from behind closed doors. It didn't mean anyone was home, though. Music playing in empty rooms was common in our house.

In the bathroom, I got undressed and hopped into the shower. The hot water relaxed me as I went over my plan. Drop the ingredients off at Mrs. Choi's restaurant at four thirty. She would show me how to clean the mussels and cook the broth. Then she would let me prep everything in her kitchen as her staff got ready for the dinner rush. Since mussels cook fast, her nice husband, Mr. Choi, would steam them and bring them to the shop in a lidded pot around seven o'clock, which would give the broth time to simmer. All I had to do was set up a folding table, a couple of chairs, a table-cloth, plates, and some cutlery, all of which Uncle Bear made me promise would be clean. A Sam-proof plan if there ever was one.

I dried off and threw on some clothes. A black T-shirt underneath a nice button-up shirt and the least wrinkly jeans I could scrounge up. With one look in the mirror, my confidence nosedived. I could see how Kyle and the other students saw me, how unimpressive I was. My body had no real shape, my nose and ears were too big for my face, and my eyes were kind of far apart. My cheeks were red from acne and the hot water. I didn't make a nice package.

Bury those thoughts, Sam. Not today.

I tossed some clothes into my backpack on top of my dinner ingredients and rushed downstairs, wanting to hit the road before anyone came home. I was steps from the door when I heard an even voice say, "Sam."

My dad was in the living room, sitting on the couch, which faced the front hallway. I hadn't noticed him. On his knee rested a glass holding a shallow layer of whisky and two ice cubes. He was always one of two men: a man who moved invisibly through the house or a hurricane on the horizon. Both terrified me.

"Why are you home?" I asked, caught off guard. He was rarely home during the day.

"I left work early so I could get to your brother's hockey game on time," he said, his voice already scolding. He tilted his head to examine me. "No school today?"

"I had last period off," I said.

Lying was the quickest way out of this conversation, but he didn't seem to buy it.

"Where are you off to?" he asked.

"Uncle Bear's."

My dad became annoyed at any mention of his brother-in-law. He put the glass down and leaned forward. With his face captured in the lamplight, I could see his bloodshot, loveless eyes.

"Sam, what are you doing?" When he spoke to me, his voice was always an octave higher than it was when he spoke to any of my siblings. "Stop wasting your time with that childish stuff. Your grades are embarrassing and you spend all your time at some stupid hobby store. You need to be a man."

His words hurt, and with every sentence that hurt deepened. I couldn't raise my head to look at him.

"I wish I knew how to help you," he said.

His rants always felt rehearsed, as if he practised them while straightening his tie every morning. He called me aimless. He said that no one wanted me and that the sphere of rejection I lived within would eventually grow to include universities and potential employers. In his eyes, it would never stop expanding. He had this habit of berating us with rhetorical or accusatory questions, so that most family dinners felt like another courtroom for him to perform cross-examinations in. This conversation was no different.

"You want to be a nothing your whole life?" he asked. He always said *a nothing* instead of just *nothing*, adding his own personal touch to the insult. Or maybe he was just repeating what he had been called when he was my age.

I'd never met my grandfather — he died two months before I was born — but I'd heard he was a tough man. He loved to tell my dad — his son — how he'd never amount to a hill of beans (the measure of success in my grandfather's day). And he'd say that if my dad ever did find a wife, good luck supporting a family with no work ethic, smarts, or talent. Even a casual observer could see that my dad wasn't in love with being a husband or a father or a lawyer. His life's purpose was to combat his own feeling of being a nothing. He lived his life as an act of rebellion against his dad. I never wanted to be like him.

"Well, the exchange program said there were certain things I could do —"

I cut myself off, knowing that every word would be more ammunition for him. I could hear how unconvincing I sounded.

"Those programs are meant for young people like Harper or kids with a lot of achievements. A year in Paris is a reward."

My only defence was my uncle's belief in me, but when I said this, my dad slammed his hand on the table, shaking the coasters. He ran his fingers through his hair as if it would help sharpen his insults. I clutched the doorknob, ready to leave. I could feel my face getting hot.

"You are not your uncle," he said, emphasizing every word. "Those stories of his are just crap he made up to entertain people polite enough to listen. There's no future for you there."

He let out a guttural sigh of frustration. He got up and walked through the dining room to the kitchen. His gait was wobbly, and a series of hiccups caused him to pat his chest. While he was distracted, I bolted from the house.

I turned my bike so sharply onto King Street that the back tire almost gave out. I was a welter of emotions. I could say that I hated my dad, but the truth was I didn't. I wanted him to appreciate me, to treat me the same as my siblings.

As I pedalled, the street signs sounded off in my head: *Victoria Street, Yonge Street, Bay Street, York Street,*

University Avenue. Every block between me and my home made me feel freer. I didn't care if I never went back. There was nothing there for me.

I waited in the alley, where cooks and servers sat smoking cigarettes, until Mr. Choi appeared. He led me into the kitchen, where Mrs. Choi was lifting a heavy pot of water onto a red burner. I spent the next hour surrounded by lemon carcasses and the skins of onions and garlic. I chopped herbs and vegetables and listened to Mrs. Choi run her kitchen like a military operation. Every ten minutes, she would check on me, grabbing the knife from my hand to show me how to properly chop the different types of vegetables.

Once I got everything flavoured and simmering to the Chois' approval, I went upstairs to Cloaked Atlas and started to set up the room. Guided by my uncle's voice in my head, which kept repeating "Ambience, Sam," I gave the place a serious sweeping, ridding it of dust bunnies that were growing their own dust bunnies. Then I dragged a poker table to the bay window that framed the view of the busy street and dropped a white tablecloth on top to cover the stained green felt. A chair on each side, a candle half-melted into a dried blob of wax between two table settings and I was done. I put on some more deodorant, rolled some lint off my shirt, and slapped way too much cologne on my neck. It was almost seven o'clock, which meant Harper would be arriving any minute.

I sat in the chair, staring out at the darkening city, trying to shoot dead the butterflies fluttering in my stomach. I watched happy couples and loving families make their way inside the shops and restaurants. A few stragglers hopped onto streetcars that then drove off in opposite directions. The energy of the city soothed me, as it always did. I grew up in a room that faced the expressway. Aaron and I would lean out the window, forearms perched on the sill, and count the cars that zipped in a never-ending stream between the half-demolished buildings that looked like chipped teeth. We would each choose a colour, and the one who counted the most cars of their colour won the game.

I was trying to think of anything besides the different ways this night could go south. It wasn't like I was going to ask her to dump her Paris plan, but maybe if I told her how I felt, we could put in some extra effort to stay in touch. Or maybe we could do a long-distance relationship for a year — that wouldn't be so bad. I could even save up some money and visit her. Or maybe I would just get that one moment I'd imagined a million times. I promised myself that whatever happened, I was going to do something.

You got this.

I was so lost in a daydream that I didn't hear the bell over the door. I eventually turned to find Harper leaning against the doorjamb, staring at me, her smile hinting at sadness. She was perfectly dressed in a green zip-up hoodie and jeans, some of her hair clipped at the back of her head.

"I didn't know it was going to be so fancy," she said.

"I'm a fancy guy."

"Those ramen noodle containers I always find in your bed are really fancy."

I got up and pulled out her chair. She seemed taken aback by my refinement, but that was the point. Tonight had to be different. I had to be different.

A minute later, Mr. Choi arrived in the elevator. He placed the steaming pot between me and Harper and ran back to his waiting customers.

"Smells amazing. You did this?"

"Of course!"

I ladled some mussels into her bowl. She picked up an empty shell and used it to extract more mussels from their shells.

"So what's the plan?"

"The plan, right. I was thinking we'd eat this meal I spent all day preparing — no big deal — and then watch *House of Usher*."

"Vinnie P.," Harper said, nodding her approval.

The moment felt right, but I still couldn't bring myself to spill my guts. Instead, we ate in awkward silence, sneaking quick glances at each other. Why did words have so much trouble leaving my mouth? It was probably because Harper was like a unicorn: smart and beautiful and kind and tough and adored by all. Even acne somehow agreed with her.

Harper mercifully broke the silence. "Hey, remember when Marco Vogelli got kicked off the bus for looking up my skirt?"

"Yup," I said with disgust. "Perv."

"And you got suspended when you told the principal that you punched him, even though it was me."

"That's right," I said.

"You did good, Sam."

We exchanged smiles, then went back to our food.

"What made you think of him?"

"I heard he's also going on the Paris exchange," she said, and my mood soured. We chewed in silence for a couple of minutes.

"I think we should talk about Kyle and what happened," Harper said, suddenly serious. She leaned back in her chair.

"I really don't want to."

"Well, I don't want to leave knowing that it hasn't been dealt with," she said.

"Then don't leave," I said.

"Sam."

"Listen, I'd really like to spend a night with you and not talk about school or Kyle or whatever," I said. "Is there any way you'd drop this?"

"No."

"Maybe we should watch the movie," I said, annoyed, feeling like the night was slipping away.

"I'll give you two options," Harper said, holding up two fingers in a peace sign. "You get to choose how the rest of the night goes."

"Deal."

"We can sit here and talk about what happened, and it'll probably lead to talking about your dad and the future or …" She trailed off playfully to build suspense.

I shook my head.

"Or …" She pointed to the office at the far end of the shop and lifted her eyebrows. At first, I didn't understand, but then I got it. She was offering me a way out of a conversation I desperately didn't want to have. The price was my uncle's private collection and, more severely, breaking a childhood pledge.

"I guess watching a movie is off the table," I said.

A conspiratorial smirk. Her answer was clear.

The desk scraped across the floor as we pulled it out from the wall. Then we squeezed around it to reach the door. I gripped the doorknob in my sweaty palm. I was about to turn it when Harper grabbed my wrist and shouted, "Wait!" I froze.

"Last chance to talk about your feelings instead of betraying your uncle," she said.

I turned the knob and the door cracked open, a sliver of black between it and the wall. I slowly opened the door all the way. It was impossible to see what was on the other side, so we just stared into the darkness of the still room.

"If Uncle Bear asks, you knocked me out just before I had a chance to stop you," I said.

"Me first," Harper said, stepping past me, half swallowed by darkness. She uttered a sincere "Whoa" before she took another step and was swallowed whole. The opening was a siren call, but I was too scared to answer. It was quiet, eerie really, until Harper called me, excited by whatever it was she saw. I took a deep breath and entered.

The shutters over the rose window created blades of moonlight that slashed the dark. Harper was flipping through some framed oil paintings that were leaning against a wall in the corner. Dangling in front of me was a metal cord. I pulled it and a bare bulb filled the room with dim light.

The small room felt like a forgotten tomb. It was underwhelming, but only because my imagination had built it up to be a sultan's treasure room that sparkled with jewels and gems. Really, though, it was just an old storage room, nothing special, with a few ragged boxes on the floor and ringed by uneven shelves lined with books and forgotten objects.

"Look at this," Harper said, holding up a blue crushed-velvet box. As she lifted the lid, the old gears in the box turned, and their achy joints expelled a soft song. I listened to the melody as I studied a shelf of smoking pipes, some long, some thick, and several hand-painted.

Thick leather-bound spines faced me at eye level, each a dark shade of black, ruby red, midnight blue, burnt orange, or forest green. *The Book of Camio*, *The Book of Gary*, *The Book of Dorian*, *The Book of Gutsmith*, *The Book of Dashiell*, *The Book of Ardat*, *The Book of Gorgora*, *The Book of Evelynn*.

"I know these books," I said, remembering that more than anything, Uncle Bear loved a great story. To him, stories were the rings of a tree that told of one's age and experience. He used to read to me, until I learned to read well enough that we could read together. First it was Narnia. Then Middle Earth, with a few Marvel Comics here and there. Finally, we found our passion with The Books of Hell.

My uncle shared these stories with me to dull the noise of the world. They muted every bully and criticism, and each adventure that drifted into my ears was like the foamy ocean washing cool sand onto my feet. Rough gym classes were met with the story of Gutsmith, a reminder that perseverance trumped easy victory. When Harper developed a crush on some lifeguard with biceps bigger than my head, Uncle Bear told me the story of Ardat versus Balthazar — Hell's David and Goliath. When I felt stupid, he would recount stories of the Leper Monks, who were all-seeing and all-knowing but were burdened by their knowledge. And when life became overwhelming, it was always Stolas. A shining example that a nothing could become a king and that a king could be kind.

"They're adventure stories," I told Harper, pulling *The Book of Dashiell* from the shelf. "I think my uncle always thought they would inspire me."

"Little did he know you'd grow up to love *Twilight*," she said.

"We were all a bit surprised by that," I replied.

"Were we, though?"

I shook my head. Harper smiled as she bent down and opened the four flaps of a box, releasing a musty smell that mixed with the stale air. She rummaged through the box, pulling out some more books, a gold platter, some rolled-up maps, a rusted sundial, and finally, a brass doorknocker that hung from the nose of a snarling demon. None of these objects made any sense.

"It's like your uncle didn't want his weird stuff to be offended by his even weirder stuff," Harper said.

As I looked at her I was hit by a tidal wave of emotion. The way the moonlight played with her hair, and that mischievous smile that revealed teeth straightened by two years of braces. I had to tell her. There wasn't going to be a better time.

"Harper," I said. "There's something I want to tell you. Ever since we were kids —"

I stopped, startled by a distant ding.

Figuring it was just Mr. Choi coming to pick up the pot, I left Harper and headed back to the showroom, where I was greeted by a smiling salesman.

MAURICE LOCKE

"Hi," I said. "Can I help you?"

"Pleasant evening," he said in a thick southern accent, every word stretched and slowed as if dripping with molasses.

"Yeah, I guess. Are you looking for my uncle?"

The man's eyes searched the room. He was tall and wore a cream-coloured suit with a red pocket square. He had slicked-back hair and a five-o'clock shadow and was carrying a black briefcase. He handed me a business card.

MAURICE LOCKE
PURVEYOR OF AUTHENTIC GOODS

"My uncle isn't here, but I'll give him your card."

"Maybe I could show you what I've brought. You never know, could be of interest."

He wandered a bit, examining the details of the shop. He stopped at the cash register and plunked his briefcase on the counter. With two simultaneous clicks he unlocked the case, then propped the top open and stepped aside to reveal its contents — or, I should say, content. Inside his briefcase was a solitary box.

"You have a box inside a box?"

"I suppose I do," he said, trying to hide his smile. Most salespeople saw me as a mark but I was used to it. "You're a very astute young man. The question, though, is what does the box inside the box hold?"

He pulled the box out of the briefcase and placed it in my outstretched hands. It was small and dark brown. Hand-carved on the top was an unsettling image. A demon gripped a young girl in its teeth. She struggled to escape, her body twisted like a helix, as they fell into a pit of fire.

"A Hanbi demon," I said, referring to the painted figure whose white skin and red eyes were unmistakable.

"You're familiar with the stories of Hell, I see," Maurice said, obviously impressed. "I don't come across that a lot."

"I grew up with them. My uncle's a bit of an expert."

I studied all the sides of the box, noting the Latin inscription written on the bottom. I went to lift the top, but Maurice placed his fingers on it to keep it shut.

Just then, there was a disturbance in the back. Harper must have knocked something over. Maurice turned his head.

"I should probably get back to my friend," I said. "I'll tell my uncle you stopped by. He might be interested in your box. He likes boxes." I expected him to apply some sales pressure, but he relented.

"You have a guest?"

"Yeah, and I really should get back to her," I said, trying not to be rude.

He looked toward the office as if he could see through the wall and into the room where Harper was rummaging around. His eyes narrowed.

"A pretty young girl, I bet," he said, bringing his gaze back to me.

I didn't reply, feeling a bit awkward and hoping Maurice would take the hint and leave.

"Takes me back, Sam," he said wistfully.

"How do you know my name?"

A feeling that something wasn't right formed in the pit of my stomach.

"I saw the photo of you on the cash register."

I looked at the cash register. Taped to the side of the beige machine was a photo of me at a museum. "Sam's 8th birthday," it read in block letters. When I was a kid, my uncle would take me out for a special birthday adventure every year. It was to replace a party with friends and whatever.

"Unrequited love," he said, brushing back his hair, which kept falling in his face. "Begging for courage we know we don't possess. Trying to say those words, not knowing if they'll be returned. Being destroyed when they are not."

He leaned against the counter, rhythmically slapping his hands on the wood. I hung my head, thinking about what he had just said. For days now, I had imagined Harper's response to my declaration of love, and each time it ended with her softly letting me down. I also knew that putting my feelings out there could make staying friends impossible, but the gnawing wouldn't go away. An itch needs to be scratched.

"You seem like a good, kind person," he said. "And good, kind people, like yourself, should get what they desire. You should be rewarded. If you're willing, I can help you."

"How?"

"With a gift."

He opened the lid to the box, which was still in my hands. Inside was a modest necklace, a thin chain holding a small circle of scratched gold with a curved sword welded on top. I can't explain it, but the necklace looked like it was glowing, a faint brightness that blanketed it and pulsed like a heartbeat. He carefully removed the necklace from the box, closed the lid, and placed it on top.

"Is it glowing?" I asked.

"The most precious metals shine the brightest," he said. "This piece was made of the rarest gold. Don't mind that it looks like someone took a sack of doorknobs to it and that the clasp is broken. It has great meaning."

The necklace looked old, which made it seem valuable and rich with history. Maurice placed a hand on my shoulder.

"Etched on this box is the most beautiful poem, the words ripped from a poet's heart. Read it to her, give her the necklace, and tell her how you feel."

"You really think this will work?"

"This necklace was not crafted to fail its owner."

He closed his briefcase and stood there, his thumb hooked in his belt loop. I wasn't sure what to say, but I was too intrigued to not give it a shot. Let's be honest, I had gone as far as I could with mussels.

I reached into my pocket for my wallet and said, "How much?"

Before Maurice could answer, my attention shifted to the office. Harper was calling my name as she made her way around the desk, on her way to the showroom. I turned back, and to my amazement, Maurice was gone. No footsteps or the sound of the front door swinging open or slamming shut.

Harper walked up to me, a look of relief on her face. I snuck the necklace into my pocket, hoping she hadn't seen it.

"You've been gone forever," she said, huffing a bit from having rushed to find me. "I was worried."

"I'm okay, was just chatting with Mr. Choi. You know how he likes to talk."

Harper laughed because Mr. Choi communicated in a series of grunts and nods. I think he once said "Bird" while looking at the sky, but I might have just imagined it.

"What's with the box?" she said.

"Oh yeah, get a load of this." I turned it over. "*Daemonium Alchem largitur sua munera.*"

I gave Harper a sly smile, a look-at-me, I-just-read-Latin kind of smile. I placed the box on the counter.

"Very impressive," she said, laughing. "Any idea what it means?"

"Not a clue."

"I'm starting to think you don't actually speak Latin," she said sarcastically.

Harper walked to the window and stared out onto the street. I stood next to her, pensive.

"I'm going to miss you," I said.

She looked at me, tucking an errant strand of hair behind her ear. I bit my bottom lip, waiting for a reply. Oh, wow, was I sweating.

"I love you," she said. The most unmistakable sentence in the English language, and she said it without hesitation.

My world tilted. There was a thrum in my ears. I didn't know what to say, but it didn't matter because words wouldn't have been able to escape my bone-dry throat. The line between my brain and my mouth had severed.

I pulled out the necklace but kept it hidden in my hand. Despite what she'd said, my mind kept enacting scenes of her rejecting me and this turning out to be our last night together. Years down the road, I'd see her in the window of a coffee shop with someone else. We'd pretend not to notice each other. I couldn't let that happen.

I pushed every bad thought out of my mind. Ignoring the potential consequences, I dangled the necklace in front of her, instantly catching her eye.

"What's this?"

"It's for you."

Her big smile matched her big eyes as I placed the necklace in her cupped hands.

"It's glowing," Harper said, her face illuminated.

"Yeah, it's rare gold, or maybe it's magic." I moved my hand like a magician waving a wand. She laughed.

"Can you help me put it on?"

"Actually, the clasp is broken. I'll get it fixed," I said.

She looked at the necklace one more time before putting it in her hoodie pocket. "I love it, Sam."

And I love you, Maurice!

The tension in the room relaxed enough that I felt comfortable taking her hand in mine. I counted to ten in my head, which I now realize is way too long to go without talking after such an intimate gesture.

"Listen, Harper, I know this might sound crazy ... or maybe it won't, but, well, I was ... I've been thinking."

She laughed at my nervousness, the way the words wobbled out of my mouth. She tightened her grip on my hand, perhaps trying to stop them from shaking. I closed my eyes.

"Ever since we were kids —" I started, but I was interrupted by a sound. A rattle, followed by a chill that passed through the room and down my spine. I opened my eyes. Harper was looking off to the side.

"Why is that box vibrating?" she asked.

"Huh?"

"Look," she said with a tremble that matched her hands.

On the counter, the box was jumping back and forth like water sizzling on a hot pan. It fell on the floor right side up. We took a few steps back. She stretched her arm in front of me, shielding me from whatever was about to happen.

The box stopped moving.

"That was weird," I said, my voice cracking.

"We should go get your uncle or something," she said.

I kneeled in front of the box. Strands of red fog seeped out of the crack where the lid closed. I was too curious to run; I had never seen anything like it before. I opened the box a touch, but as I did, the red fog threw the lid open. It came out faster and faster, rising to the ceiling and then rappelling down the walls. The shop turned a dark shade of red.

We slowly stepped back until we were against the window. Harper's eyes were as big as saucers. My jaw dropped, and all my joints felt locked. I looked toward the exit, the only way out.

Before us, the fog outlined a door that framed a town beneath a sky lacquered red. Curiosity pinned us.

"Holy shit!" I said.

"What is this?" Harper said, her voice tense and low.

The box was a projector, the room a dark theatre, and we the sole audience members looking at a desolate, quiet town where wood buildings lined an empty dirt road.

"We should go," I said.

Paralyzed by an emotion somewhere between awe and fear, we couldn't run or look away. Harper, always the brave one, reached in. Just as her hand was about to cross the doorway, I grabbed her wrist and pulled it back.

"What are you doing?" I said.

"It's amazing," she said. "It looks real."

The fog started to move aggressively, slightly breaking the shape of its door. Wisps floated around the room, knocking things off shelves and shaking the walls and cases. Glass shattered, displays toppled, books and objects fell off the shelves. I squeezed Harper's hand, unable to process what was happening.

As the fog inched toward us, it grew thicker, forming what looked like a hand ready to clutch.

"Run!" I said.

I pulled Harper with me as I broke toward the front door, more scared than I had ever been in my life. I had almost reached it when I was yanked back, her hand slipping from mine. Harper was lying on her stomach, the red fog wrapped around her ankle. She was being pulled in the direction of the box, screaming as tears streamed down her flushed cheeks. I ran after her, dived onto my stomach and latched on to her hands. But the force pulling her was too strong and, once again, she slipped away.

Do something.

I ran to close the lid of the box, but as soon as I touched it, I was thrown through the air as if a large fist had rammed my chest. I smashed against a bookcase with a hard *oomph*. Dizzy, I lifted my head, and through the legs of stands and tables I saw Harper, desperately clawing at the floor. The force lifted her, and, like a ruthless magic trick, her legs vanished through the doorway. She screamed my name, her voice hoarse, until the very last second when her head crossed the threshold.

The box slammed shut.

The red fog was gone.

The town with the red sky was gone.

Harper was gone.

I was shaking in the corner, drenched in sweat, when they found me. All I could do was stutter a few bits of nonsense. I tried to focus my sight, but my eyes felt like two loose marbles. Raymond and my uncle helped me up and sat me in a chair. Their expressions were a mix of concern and shock, made worse by my inability to respond to their questions.

"Sam, are you okay?" Uncle Bear asked, scanning the disaster zone of his shop.

"What happened?" Raymond leaned in closer. "Were we robbed?" He pushed his glasses up the bridge of his nose. He was a bit younger than my uncle, with a head of untameable hair and a groomed moustache. He spoke with a British accent.

"Sam," Uncle Bear steadied my chin with his hand to stop my eyes from shifting. "Where's Harper?"

"She's gone," I said, my voice barely audible. It felt like I was coming out of anesthesia.

Raymond and Uncle Bear shared a quizzical look.

"I'm sorry. I'm sorry. He gave me a box and then the fog and … and … it took her," I rambled.

"Slow down. What box?" Raymond threw his arms up in confusion. I pointed to the box sitting innocently on the floor. My uncle wheeled over, picked it up, and placed it on his lap.

"I've never seen this before," he said as he returned to us. "Where did you find this?"

I pulled out Maurice's business card and handed it to Raymond. His face soured. He handed the card to my uncle, who, upon reading the name, sank in his chair.

"You went into the room," my uncle said.

I replied with a guilty nod.

"I told you to get a lock for it," Raymond said.

"I thought a promise was stronger than a lock," my uncle said, his eyes betraying his disappointment.

He rolled into his office. He must have seen the open door, because he screamed a curse word, something I had never heard him do before. Raymond removed his blazer and placed it around my shoulders to stop my shaking.

Uncle Bear returned with a book and the music box.

"Sam, did you open this music box?"

"Harper did," I said.

They looked at each other.

"Oh boy," my uncle said.

I kept apologizing to them. Quickly, their anger shifted to pity. My uncle patted my arm and Raymond rubbed my back. There was something they weren't telling me, and I was starting to feel even more scared.

"Is she dead?"

My question was ignored. Raymond retreated to the office, and a moment later I could hear him moving things around.

Uncle Bear picked up the thick brown book and flipped the pages until he reached the middle. He showed me a black-and-white drawing of a thin Hanbi hiding behind a curtain, watching a small boy. I could see the demon's sinister smile and dark beady eyes. In gothic font, the caption read, "Moloch the Trickster."

"This is the real Maurice Locke," he said. "Did he meet Harper?"

"No," I said, replaying the events in my head. "But I think he heard her."

"I'm sorry, Sam. This is all my fault." My uncle's eyes welled as he rubbed his chin.

I had no idea what was going on. I wasn't even sure if Harper was still alive. All I knew was that there was a salesman who, according to some book, was a demon and that the room refused to stop closing in on me.

Raymond called us to join him. We entered the office, where Raymond had placed a book, a scrolled parchment, and a transparent sheet on the desk.

"There's no easy way to say this, Sam. Harper was brought to another world, one very far away and much different from our own," Raymond said.

"But one that you know, Sam," Uncle Bear said. His voice sounded like a rope splintered a hundred times. His eyes were bleak.

We all sat in silence. I didn't know what to say.

Finally, my uncle continued. "Remember the stories I used to tell you?"

"About Middle Earth?"

"About Hell," Uncle Bear said. I felt as if lightning should have crashed as he said it, but it was a clear and balmy night.

"Hell? But those were just bedtime stories."

Uncle Bear and Raymond exchanged sideway glances. The room was so tense, it felt like a geyser ready to blow. Raymond unfurled the scroll, revealing a map with frayed edges. It looked as if it had been dipped in tea and turmeric. Some lazy cartographer had drawn only a few squiggly lines as mountains and rivers and scribbled a handful of town names here and there.

"I think you should sit down and take a few deep breaths," Uncle Bear said to me. "Things are about to get weird."

I took a seat and dropped the blazer from my shoulders. Suddenly, I felt sick.

"This is going to be hard to believe, but every word is true," Raymond said. He looked to my uncle and signalled with his eyes for him to take the baton. Uncle Bear jumped right in.

"Tonight you were visited by a demon named Moloch. I'm sorry to say this, but Harper brought him here. By accident, of course. The song from the music box guided him to our front door."

"Which is why it should have been destroyed," Raymond interjected.

"You don't destroy valuable artifacts from other worlds," Uncle Bear said through clenched teeth.

Raymond rolled his eyes. Clearly, they'd had this conversation before.

Uncle Bear continued. "He saw an opportunity to take advantage of you. He most likely sought a Berdymian."

It all started to come back to me, one drip at a time. The Books of Hell spoke of our world. They didn't call it Earth, because they had no sense of our world as a spinning blue and green rock in the vast canvas of space. They didn't know about continents or countries, either, and probably didn't care about our oceans. They knew it as one big world, Berdym.

"You guys have been knocking back the absinthe again, right? I won't judge."

"Yes, we have. But Sam, this is serious," Uncle Bear said.

"I know it is! My best friend is missing and you're telling me about demons."

"Then listen to me. Every story I told you was true."

Frustrated, I rubbed my face, feeling tense all the way to my fingertips and wanting to scream. Everything that happened after Maurice had disappeared was beyond belief, but two people I trusted were trying to convince me otherwise.

"Think about what happened tonight," Uncle Bear said.

He was right. There was no logical explanation except that something extraordinary, something beyond human reason, was at play.

"Hell is an intersection of a hundred thousand worlds that exist beyond our own," Raymond said. He took the transparent sheet and placed it over the map, lining up the corners. The map was transformed from a few towns linked by dotted dirt roads to a rich world spreading right to the edges of the tattered paper. I held my breath as I took in Hell's landscape.

"Ooooookay," I said.

"The box is one of Alchem's Gifts. The design looks Alpsecordian, so my guess is Harper was brought to Mara," Uncle Bear said, his finger hovering over a town on the map that neighboured a mountain. A mountain that existed in Hell.

Everything Uncle Bear and Raymond said and argued about, and they did argue a lot that night, swooped in and then out of my brain. It was gibberish that carried on for hours. Or maybe it wasn't. How would one even start to process something like that? I had no idea. How would you feel if you learned that Mother Goose ate children? Or that Humpty Dumpty was an evil ruler? Or that Cinderella liked to stab people? That's how I felt as I spent the rest of that night learning that the fairy tales of my youth were real and that Hell was a world where demons lived and where people — Berdymians — were taken. I heard words and names that I hadn't thought about in years, things I thought were imaginary. Every detail gutted me while simultaneously confirming my fear.

Despite my skepticism, there was one fact that was indisputable.

Harper was in serious trouble. And it was all my fault.

4
THE PLAN

That night ended with a plan. My uncle made a list of thirteen people who had travelled to Hell to explore or to make a reode (a buck in Hell's currency). Raymond probably regretted mentioning that over the centuries, thousands upon thousands of people had been taken against their will. None had ever come back.

The one card up our sleeve was that we had one of the rare boxes that could open a doorway to that world. We just needed to find the right person daring enough to go through it.

Of the thirteen people on the list, seven had never been heard from again and three were known to have died on their journey. This left three. Uncle Bear would contact them, offering a reward if they were willing to take on our mission. The first two hung up the phone before he could make the offer. The last one told us to write her a sweet epitaph and move on. So much for that plan.

Things were not moving fast enough. While I waited for Uncle Bear to get off the phone, I made a big mistake and started rereading passages from The Books of Hell. They reminded me that not only was Harper missing, but she was also in an alien world that was best described as chaotic and dangerous. Horrible thoughts consumed me, not just that she might be in pain or dead, but that she was alone and scared, feelings I understood.

I found Harper's phone in the middle of the show-room. It must have fallen out of her pocket the night she disappeared. Posing as Harper, I texted her parents, telling them that she was going to spend a few days at a friend's place preparing for Paris. I even outlined an itinerary. It was the only thing I could do to buy some time. The next day they called the shop looking for her. Luckily, Uncle Bear assured Mrs. James that Harper was spending some time with me and that he would pass on the message.

We were running out of time. Either we had to come clean to Harper's parents and the police, which would have resulted in me being put in a mental hospital and Uncle Bear in prison, or we had to figure out a way to bring her home. We needed help.

With Harper missing, I wandered around like a ghost, a husk incapable of feeling anything besides anguish. Once a bit of the shock wore off, the pain set in, so intense it took my breath away. When a wave of emotion hit, I had to find an empty alley or room where I could hunch over and let it pass over me. I missed her so much.

Two days after Harper disappeared, I put in a full day at school so the secretary wouldn't call my parents, and even made an appearance at home to erase any suspicion. My mom gave me a hug when she saw me. It was obvious she had spoken with my dad, because she reassured me that I could spend as much time with my uncle as I wanted. She also made me stay for dinner, which was an awkward hour where the only sound was my dad grilling Amy about the bar exam. I couldn't wait to get out of there.

When I returned to the shop, the office door was partway open. I peered inside to see that Raymond and my uncle were having a conversation. I stood quietly on the other side of the wall as they, not realizing I was there, debated whether I had what it took to go on the mission. My uncle kept emphasizing that I was only sixteen years old, meaning too young and inexperienced.

"You were only fifteen when you hopped the rails to California," Raymond reminded him.

A bottle clinked against the lip of a glass. They were three-quarters of the way through a bottle of W.L. Weller twelve-year-old bourbon. They kept reviewing every possible solution, but each was a dead end. It got to the point that Raymond offered to go, but given that he had diabetes and needed to nap while watching *Dr. Phil*, he probably wasn't the best choice.

My heart lurched when my uncle started speaking nostalgically about Harper. He had known her since she was very young and always thought she was special. Now, though, he was speaking about her as if she was already dead. He sighed heavily just before he admitted that their greatest fear might have been realized. Harper might be lost forever.

I went to my room, which felt smaller than it was. I turned the lights off and lay in bed, staring at the ceiling, where Harper and I had created a Milky Way of glow-in-the-dark stars. It was cheesy, but we liked lying there and staring at it while we planned our future, which was always Kyle-less and rejection-free. I guess it was more fantasizing than planning, but I already missed those moments. They made me feel like there was something better out there, a place where I wasn't a total loser.

The glow from the ceiling illuminated my night table, on which was stacked a short tower of books. In between two textbooks was *The Book of Stolas*. I pulled it out and an idea struck me like a hammer to my head. I sat up and started flipping through some passages. Stolas was a warrior, a winner, a daring adventurer, a leader. If Hell was real — and I now had no choice but to admit it was — then so was Stolas. In my hand I held the clues to find him, and from there all I'd have to do was convince him to help me. Stolas was the answer.

I rushed into the office, surprising Uncle Bear and Raymond. I dropped *The Book of Stolas* onto the map of Hell, next to the town of Mara, which was circled in coffee.

"Stolas," I said.

"Mrs. Goldenberg's dog?" Uncle Bear replied, confused.

"No, that's Samson," I said, pacing in a circle. "You're telling me that demons and Hell are real. So that means that Stolas is real. If I find him, he can help me."

The smallest spark of confidence started to grow inside of me, only to be extinguished when my uncle pushed the book toward me and told me to forget it.

"Why? He's perfect. He did all these heroic —"

My uncle cut me off with a wave of his hand. *Not a chance*, his expression said.

"Why not?"

"That book was written before his story was finished. Do you know what happened to him?" Before I could speak, he answered his own question. "He was betrayed and sentenced to a terrible place called the Mines of Belphegor. So even if your going was a good idea — and it's not — he is not the answer."

He lifted his eyebrows, and for a split second I saw the resemblance between him and my mom. Raymond kept swivelling his head between the two of us. I'd never fought with my uncle before. There hadn't been a single moment when he was anything less than my biggest supporter. But right now, he didn't believe in me.

"I can do this," I said.

"Think about it. First, you would have to make it from Mara to Belphegor."

The map showed that Belphegor wasn't far from Mara, but for all I knew there were a thousand pits of fire and an angry army of flesh-eating demons between the two. Fair point.

"Then you would have to find Stolas in the mines, which are protected by Banshees. From there, you would have to escape the falling city and make it through a territory patrolled by the Wanderers," he said. "Remember the stories about the Wanderers? Oh, there's also the whole bringing-him-back-to-life issue."

"What if he found a Leper Monk?" Raymond said. My uncle shot him a dirty look. He replied in kind.

"There are very few left, and by law they rarely interfere," my uncle said.

Raymond went into the private collection room and returned holding a thin book with a blood red spine, *The Leper Monks' New Incantations.*

"One problem solved at least," Raymond said. "We bought this book from a reputable dealer in Zaire. No guarantees but most find its contents trustworthy."

My uncle looked like his head was about to explode. "Sam, there's no one in any world who is perfectly good," he said. "I'm begging you to drop this."

"You don't think I can do this," I said. My uncle was viewing me the same way my dad and the kids at school did. A loser, too scared to take a chance, incapable of anything heroic.

"I have always believed that you can do anything, you know that," he said. "But I can't risk your life. You're too important to me."

Something stirred in me, a foreign feeling. Determination.

"Then what are we going to do?" I said, frustrated by the lack of a solution, one so obviously right that my uncle would set it in motion and I could relax, knowing that Harper would safely return home.

"We're working on it," Uncle Bear said.

That wasn't good enough for me.

The Leper Monks' New Incantations. Check.

The map. Check.

The stupid box. Check.

Fruit leather. Check.

A hunting knife. Check. *Hope it's sharp.* I pricked my finger on the tip. *Yup, sharp.*

Except for Maurice's box, which I held in my hands, I had placed all those items in a backpack. I walked to the middle of the shop, which was once again lit by moonlight. I read the inscription on the box.

As I waited, I was brought back to a few nights earlier, when Harper was ripped from my life. I was branded by the memory and could hear her hoarse voice right next to me, whispering in my ear.

I left a note on the counter explaining that this was my only choice. And that whatever happened, I alone was responsible for this decision. I'd outlined the lack of options and said that it was clear that the only two people who would even consider risking their lives for this mission weren't physically able to. There was no one else. And I knew one fact that would haunt me forever if I did nothing: Harper would have searched to the ends of any world to find me.

Go to Hell. Find Stolas. Save Harper. Come home.

Like veins and sinew, the red fog billowed out of the box. I felt the blood drain from my face just as quickly. The lid opened. Mara appeared, the same view as before. I remembered stories Uncle Bear used to tell me. Adventures in a strange world. High stakes. Heroes and villains. I remembered the battles, the waves of blood and the sound of clashing swords washing over fields and city streets. Not Toronto — Ragewick, Ep Sumter, the City of Belphegor. One story, a favourite of my uncle's, played out in my mind like a movie: Gusts of winds pushed the sails of thousands of ships across a never-ending black sea, the thick pounding of drums scoring their journey. Aboard the ships were demons anxious for a new home, to set foot upon their own Ellis Island. The early history of a new world and its settlers. I felt now as they must have felt as they crossed the rough waters gripped by some beacon.

The foggy door frame dissolved into strands. One strand was instantly attracted to me. It didn't need to clutch me like it did Harper — I was willing — but it didn't care about my needs or wants. It wrapped around my wrist and pulled me toward the dirt road on the other side.

I tucked the box under my arm as fog surrounded me, filling my vision. I steeled myself, knowing I was about to leave the only world I had ever known. Then again, most people only ever know one world.

MARA

U ncle Bear's voice was sturdy — so strong, in fact, that a perfect image of him formed in my mind. The way his arms moved as he spoke and the different voices he would drum up for different characters. His words echoed in my head like a radio play, giving me context, as useful as it was comforting.

Older than the Roman Empire is the notion that demons are merely part of Hell's fabric, a ghost story meant to scare people into following the rules. But according to The Books of Hell, demons came from many different worlds and settled in Hell, like so many humans did in our New World.

The first known settlers were the Alpsecords, the bringers of nightmares. They sprinkled ash as their border and named their home Mara, where I was now an intruder.

An armada of birds flew through the dark clouds in the crimson sky. On stark branches, black leaves shook from the movement of something I couldn't see, something I really didn't want to see. I stood on a street that ran along the edge of a cliff. I peered over the edge and found a long drop down a rocky mountain.

This is real. This is real. This isn't a dream.

My sweat-soaked shirt clung to me like a second skin, and my heart was beating fast, almost too fast. I was suddenly very aware of my few possessions. I took out the knife and tucked it into the back of my pants so only the black handle was sticking out. I would probably need it soon.

Nervous, I walked down the street, feeling as if I were trespassing on an abandoned movie set. Everything felt very different from home.

After passing a series of boarded-up shops, I stopped in front of a filthy window. I wiped some of the dirt off and saw a row of empty barber chairs, each reclined and facing a different direction. As I leaned in closer, a broom smacked the glass. I jumped back and squinted, trying to make out the blurry creature on the other side. He was pointing his grey finger, telling me to leave.

I moved on cautiously. I felt like I was wandering through the fog of a dream, the beginning of a nightmare. The wooden sidewalk creaked sharply with every step.

I looked around, taking stock of where I was. On each side of me a dirt road stretched into the distance, finally merging with the sky.

Keep moving.

A husky demon with charcoal skin and pointy ears walked on the other side of the street. He looked at me before waddling into a clapboard building that dwarfed the others.

I couldn't believe where I was. Even the temperature surprised me, a dry, sweltering heat that made the chill of Toronto a distant memory.

Okay, okay, okay, do something.

A hot breeze lifted the dirt. I stood in the middle of the street, wondering if Harper had been brought here, if she had stood in this very spot. That thought was replaced by a more pressing one: I needed some serious help. I had to stay focused and not do my usual Sam thing. I was in Hell — the first part of my plan was complete. Now on to the second. *Find Stolas.*

In front of me, between two closed shops, stood a one-storey wooden building. Through the window, I could see a demon sitting at a bar. Her smile was enough to convince me to enter.

Inside, half of the circular tables were filled with patrons enjoying drinks. Plumes of smoke from hand-rolled cigarettes trailed from mouths and nostrils, creating a blue haze that climbed the dark wooden walls.

I'm in my very first bar — and it's filled with mean-looking demons.

A demon was sitting at a table with a headless someone in a pinstripe suit. At the next table were three smaller demons. Two wore hooded robes, and the other had rough red skin and a little patch of black hair poking out of his head. A two-headed vulture hung upside down from a swaying chandelier. He pointed at me as if to let me know I didn't belong.

At the bar, I sat next to the smiling demon I had seen through the window. She had a bob haircut and chalk-white skin. She was playing with a coin, spinning it, slamming it down with her palm, spinning it again.

"Sorry to bug you, but you wouldn't happen to know how to get to Belphegor, would you?"

She turned to me and her face unfurled into four parts that folded behind her head, revealing just a gaping throat, a tongue, and two eyeballs stuffed into decayed tissue. She stepped down from the stool, grabbed me by the throat, and pushed me up against the bar.

The entire room stopped to stare at me, but their sudden interest quickly dissolved into sneers and growls. The demon finally released my throat. Instead of fighting back, I decided it was best to look down and try not to arouse any more trouble.

"Take everything he has and leave him naked in the Styx!" a voice yelled out.

Another voice lifted above the crowd. "String him from the gallows and shake his pockets."

After being in Hell for only fifteen minutes, I found myself the subject of the most terrifying brainstorming session ever. The headless one broke through the small crowd and came right up to me. I could now see that his head was situated snugly in his neck, face up, his grey eyes staring at me. It took effort to hold down my last meal.

"The Hanbi might like this one. I'd hand him over to Cerberus for a few pints," the female demon said.

"We can get a lot more than that," another proclaimed.

I slowly slipped my hand behind my back to reach for the knife, but the headless one grabbed my arm.

As I searched my mind for any hint of what I should do next, I heard a raspy voice from below. "Watch it. Watch it. I clean."

At my feet was a small demon holding a dustpan. He had a pot-belly, a hawk nose, and scraps of black hair on his head. Suspenders held up his tattered blue pants. A chain around his neck led into a trap door in the floor.

He looked up to me just before a demon kicked him away. He cowered, his expression shifting to fear.

I looked back at the crowd. Panic set in, and I felt like I was going to barf on everyone in front of me. Someone grabbed my backpack and pulled me toward the door, but after a step I was pulled the other way by a hooded demon.

"Mark my words, if we send him with Hasha, she'll be enjoying the finest brews in the closest tavern to The Spear," he said. The others grumbled in agreement. The Spear was the highest cliff in Hell. Its tip was shaped like a pointed head. Far below was a deep river. From the stories I'd read, I knew it was a popular place to carry out death sentences for criminals.

The little demon and I locked eyes. His face showed empathy. Then his eyes moved to the vulture whose talons gripped the chandelier directly above the crowd.

As the creatures in the room continued to argue, the little demon moved through the crowd, his chain dragging behind him, all the way to the back of the room. He lifted himself onto the windowsill, climbed up the curtain, and started clawing at a knotted ball of rope. His tongue was hanging out of the side of his mouth as he tried to untie the knot from the fixture. I couldn't figure out what he was doing until my eyes followed the rope to the chandelier.

"Let's all march him to the base of Mount Beleth and wait until Cerberus arrives."

"Why don't we send a cipher to Pazuzu? He can send someone to pick up this ugly thing."

"I say we take him to the next slave auction over in Ragewick and let the highest bidder fill our coffers."

"If we wait too long he'll end up like Terry, and then no one will get anything," the vulture croaked.

The suggestions made my pulse go nuts, and I couldn't help but imagine all the horrible things they were going to do to me. Still, most of my attention was focused on the determined little demon and the knot that he had just untied. He held the rope and motioned for me to move aside. I took a big step to my right.

Clever little guy, I thought.

He let go of the rope. It whizzed through every hoop that had held it in place along the wall. As the rope flew up, the chandelier came down, crushing the vulture and a table full of demons with a room-shaking bang. The crystals shattered into hundreds of shards.

I was frozen. The little demon had climbed down from the windowsill without anyone noticing what he had just done. His chain rustled across the floor, and then he appeared at the open trap door.

"C'mon, c'mon, c'mon. No Terry," he said before climbing down the hole.

I ran to the hole and stared into the dark. I could hear him mumbling. There was movement behind me as some of the demons started to rise. The idea of jumping into the unknown was terrifying, but it was my best bet.

I stepped forward but was stopped by a hand clutching my ankle. A flash of a nightmare. I was suddenly back in Cloaked Atlas. Crumpled in a shadowy corner was an emotionless Harper, still wearing her green hoodie. The shadows enveloped her. She didn't say a word as she disappeared from my view once again.

I screamed and jerked my body. The nightmare ended, and there I was, back in the tavern in Mara, my ankle held tight by a demon whose legs were victims of the fallen chandelier.

I ripped my leg from her grip, then lowered myself into the hole. I pulled the door shut, bolted the lock, and found myself shrouded in darkness.

6
THORLTON

"Can't be here. No, no, no." The little demon raced through his words.

He abruptly stopped speaking and, like a cat washing, started to lick his hand and stroke his head with it. Pacing in a circle, he looked more distressed than he had upstairs. There was a bolt holding the shackle around his neck. I pulled it out, causing the shackle to open and fall to the ground. He rubbed the deep impression on his neck and looked even more scared than before.

"Oh, no, no, no," he said.

"What's your name?" I said, following him as he started walking down the tunnel, which was dimly lit by torches. The tunnel was made of grey interlocking stones, and the walls and ceiling were covered in scratch marks. Steel bars allowed me to see into the empty cells lining both sides.

"Thorlton. Um, yeah, Thorlton."

"I'm Sam. Are we safe down here?"

"Asag, very bad demon. Very bad," he replied, constantly fidgeting with his hands.

"I don't know what that means. Why did you help me?"

Thoughts seemed to bounce around his head like a pinball. He pointed into a cell. Behind the metal bars I could see bones piled in the corner.

"Terry," he said, and I understood what he meant.

My brain felt like liquid, trying to understand how I had gone from Toronto to Hell in one day. I stopped Thorlton from walking by placing a hand on his shoulder.

"Do you know who Stolas is?"

He shook his head.

"Do you know how to get to Belphegor?"

He rubbed his chin.

"No. No."

Before I even had a chance to worry about my next move, a low rumble filled the tunnel. I turned around. In the flickering torchlight stood a dark figure. He was gaunt, with a thin face that came to a sharp point at his chin. Four horns curled in different directions. In his hand he held a chain attached to two feral creatures on all fours. Their foamy mouths shook as they growled.

"Asag, Asag," Thorlton said. His body tensed.

The chain smacked the ground, ringing loudly. The demonic dogs ran full speed up the sides of the walls and then along them, heading toward us.

We bolted down the tunnel. Claws scratched at the stone, making an awful piercing sound. Asag cackled and called out to Thorlton. The name rolled off his tongue: "Thorrrllton! Thorrrllton!"

I ran faster than I ever thought possible — which will happen when you're being chased by creatures running on walls. I sprinted past Thorlton, following the line of torches that led to a metal gate. On the other side was a refreshing green valley. I was going too fast and was too uncoordinated to stop, so I collided with the gate, causing it to shift loose as rocks and dirt fell on my head and shoulders.

Frantically, I threw my shoulder against the gate over and over, but it didn't shift enough to open. I clenched the bars that separated me from the valley. It looked safe. I would have given anything to be there, or anywhere else really.

Thorlton, screaming and waving his arms, jumped onto my backpack. The gate must have been looser than I thought, because his weight thrust both me and it forward. The dislodged gate crashed to the ground, and I, still holding on to its bars, lost my balance. My stomach dropped into my feet.

Thorlton and I were passengers on the gate as it slid down a rocky mountainside toward the valley below. My screams scared the birds out of the nearby trees. At the end of the tunnel, the demonic dogs barked as they watched us get away. Thorlton dug his nails into me and buried his head against my shoulder as we picked up speed. We were on a clear path to hit a pile of jagged rocks at the base of the mountain. I closed my eyes, but they were jarred back open as we hit a rock at top speed and were flung high in the air.

My back ached from landing on the hard ground. I slowly got to my feet and looked to Thorlton, who was lying on a flat rock.

"Oh my god! Are you okay?"

"Fine. Fine," Thorlton said. A few seconds later he rolled off the rock, found his feet, and stretched.

I felt a pang of guilt. What would have happened if I had confessed my love to Harper when we were younger and if we'd been together ever since? My life would have been different: I'd have better grades and more friends, I would have made a few teams, and now I'd be planning a year in Paris with her instead of wondering how I would ever survive a year without her. But I had never found that flash of courage.

None of that mattered now, because I was in a new world, walking next to a little demon in suspenders through a wide field of bright green and yellow grass at the base of a mountain. I was coming down from the high of escape, noticing how the air smelled so fresh, unlike the air tainted with exhaust and sweat that wafted through the streets back home. Still, I missed the street noise and the comfort of my neighbourhood.

Even though I had learned about Hell for most of my childhood, I still expected a flat world of fire and brimstone. But so far, I had already experienced a town on top of a mountain and a beautiful valley. If it weren't for the red sky, I might have convinced myself that I was simply enjoying a pleasant hike.

Thorlton's stubby legs moved as fast as his mouth as he tried to stay close to me.

"So where ya from?" I asked him.

"Don't know. Been in Mara and the tavern and the tunnels," he said. I was starting to think that Thorlton had been shackled his entire life.

"So you're an Alpsecord?"

He shook his head.

"Incubus," he corrected me. "Asag an Alpsecord. Hermann, too. Oh, and Hasha. Very bad dreams all night."

"Who?"

Using his hands, Thorlton mimicked his face opening like a flower, telling me exactly who Hasha was. He then slumped his head and deepened his voice, telling me that Hermann was the headless guy. He ended his impressions with a giggle.

I couldn't remember anything about the Incubi.

"I need to get to Belphegor and find someone named Stolas. Any idea how we can make this happen?

"Uhhhh ... Stolas? No. Oh, Belphegor! No."

It was hard not to feel frustrated, but I had to keep going. I was bound to get a break or two, right? Isn't that how it works when you take a big chance?

We continued walking for a long time.

"Is there a town nearby? Or somewhere we can stop for directions?"

"Beleth ... hmmm ... but bad. Can't go, Sam," he replied.

Before I could respond, a shadowy figure on a winged black horse streaked across the sky.

"Cerberus. Cerberus," Thorlton said in a shaky voice that filled me with anxiety.

My heart raced. We broke into a sprint, my backpack bouncing all around. Every time I thought I had reached my top speed, I found another gear. I tried to keep my eyes pointed toward the mountains, but I couldn't help staring at the flying horse, whose black body stood out against the red sky. A long piece of rope was tied to its tail, and attached to the rope were severed limbs and heads. They danced in the current of the wind as the horse glided toward us.

We hid behind an enormous boulder jutting out from the ground. I put my hand over Thorlton's mouth, and, for whatever reason, he licked me.

Cerberus's horse landed close by, still galloping. Cerberus climbed down, and I craned my head to see his hulking body. His face was all scarred flesh and pointy teeth. Two sharp black horns shot out of his head. If that wasn't terrifying enough, two more heads fanned out like peacock feathers. All six of his eyes stared at the boulder.

I focused on my breathing, trying to bring it down to a quiet level.

"You have trespassed in the valley owned by Pazuzu," Cerberus said. "If you run to the east you will reach the village of Pazuzu's birth and you will be brought to me. If you run along the Riverway, you will arrive at The Spear and be brought to stand before Pazuzu."

I remembered the name Pazuzu from the books. He was bad news. Thorlton and I looked at each other.

"Maybe we can reason with this guy," I whispered.

"No. No. Sam. Cerberus bad." Thorlton slid his finger across his throat and made a croaking sound. I gripped my knife but knew it was pointless. There was no way I could fight or outrun a three-headed demon on a flying horse.

"Come forward or the punishment will be harsh," Cerberus said.

Behind us was a shallow gully that divided the valley from a dense forest. I put my knife in my backpack so Cerberus wouldn't take it, and then carefully walked down and placed my backpack on the ground, covering it with leaves and twigs.

"Sam. Sam. Whatcha doing?" Thorlton said, doing his best to whisper, but he had only two versions of an indoor voice: loud and slightly less loud.

"Don't mention my bag. We'll come back for it," I said. Thorlton gulped.

We stepped out from behind the boulder, arms raised. Cerberus walked toward us, giving me a better look at his three menacing heads. The two smaller ones moved constantly on thin necks that protruded from the top of his back.

"I'm sorry. I didn't realize I was doing something wrong. I'm on my way to Belphegor. Any chance you can point me in the right direction?"

He smiled and narrowed his eyes.

"Of course," Cerberus said.

I don't know why, but something about his three smiling faces made me feel as if I had finally taken a step toward finding Harper.

1

PAZUZU

My body was tied to a white torso that looked as if blood hadn't flowed through it in a long time. Another thick rope that lassoed the winged horse around its haunches bound my feet. The face of an old demon kept smacking mine, making my head feel like a piñata. Thorlton was tied to a meaty thigh. He kept licking it, seeming to get some weird satisfaction from it.

We flew through the sky. The sick feeling in my stomach worsened with every second. From high above, I saw a port village, with smoke curling from chimneys as if it were being summoned to the sky. The village looked sweet and welcoming, like it belonged in a motel-room painting. I knew better than to trust what I was seeing, because that village was Beleth and it was anything but welcoming.

The horse glided lower and we braced for the landing. As we smacked into frigid swampy water, the cold sent a shock through my body. The horse dragged us along a dirt road that ran between two rows of huts, lined by torches and leading to a town square. The first thing I noticed was the gallows, where several nooses hung from the crosspiece. A message was carved into the wood: THOSE WHO DOUBT ALCHEM.

Long before Stolas and the Architects, there was Alchem, a sorcerer who ruled the Hanbi. I came across a drawing of him once. A small and withered demon, too insignificant to be memorable. His appearance, however, was an illusion, a magic trick performed by the artist.

Every race of demon had a story, a series of events that led them to Hell. The Alpsecords were chased from the Nothingness by a pestilent wind. The Krauss arrived only after a famine. The Hanbi, though, seemed to just appear one day in the woods that surround the valley.

The Hanbi were rural demons. But instead of raising a barn through community effort like people in a village might do, the Hanbi would raise it with a combination of magic and slaves. They were also a mean bunch.

Cerberus dismounted the horse and let out a grunt. He led me behind the gallows toward a large stone house that towered over the huts. Thorlton remained tied to the horse, whimpering.

A female voice shouted from inside the house. Like an apparition, the voice's owner emerged, then stormed passed us, her eyebrows arched as if trying to bury a nagging thought. I did a double take. She looked so much like the girls at my school. Her blond hair was tied in a simple ponytail. Her clothing was plain: a black long-sleeve shirt and grey pants that hid the top of her black boots. The only thing different about her was the crossbow in her hand and the quiver of arrows on her back. She threw me a disarming look as we crossed paths.

Inside, the house reeked of dead flowers. The only light came from the dancing flames in the fireplace.

Cerberus left my side and went to stand at arm's length from a dark corner. "I found this one with an Incubus in the valley outside Mara," he said.

I was confused about why he was talking to a corner until a honeyed voice called from the shadows.

"Your name?" the voice asked. Cerberus turned to look at me.

"S-Sam," I said.

A figure stepped out of the shadows, walked to the fireplace, and hunched toward the light of the fire. I recognized him immediately. It was Pazuzu.

"Why were you on my land?" he said.

I started by telling him I didn't want any trouble, then launched into an explanation about searching for my friend. I ended by saying I had no intention of sticking around and promised that as soon as I found her, I would head home. There was no acknowledgement that he cared or was even listening. His eyes didn't leave the fire, his face bathed in its orange light.

"You're Berdymian," he said.

I gave the smallest of nods, not knowing if that fact would work in my favour or not.

"And who is it you're looking for?"

"Her name's Harper. She doesn't belong here." My voice caught in my throat.

He finally turned to face me. I shrank under his gimlet eye, shocked to be in his company. His long toenails scraped the floor as he moved toward me. His white skin had grey contours that darkened to black around his baleful red eyes, making it look as if he were wearing eyeshadow, except he wasn't. His black mouth flashed a gruesome smile. His was the face children see when they are left alone in the dark. I knew from experience. When I was a kid, my parents had to buy nightlights in bulk because of the stories my uncle told me about the demon Pazuzu.

The scent of dead flowers was stronger now that he was right in front of me. He stroked my face with the back of his rough hand, then ordered Cerberus to take me to his garden and to deal with the filthy Incubus. My body ached with fear.

I was brought to a clearing, but instead of pretty flowers and underbrush, the area was filled with statues of figures that looked like they were covered in clay, all posed in unnatural ways. One was leaning forward, its jaw lowered, as if frozen in the middle of a frightful scream. Another was lying on the ground, back arched as if it were being electrocuted. Several hung upside down from trees. I was scared. Terrified, actually.

"What is this?" I asked.

Cerberus grabbed me by my shoulders and shoved me between two columns. Clay bubbled up from the ground and covered my feet, then made its way up my legs and stomach, and, finally, muffled my screams as it covered my head. I was helpless, stuck in a straightjacket of hardened mud.

I was trapped inside this nightmare for hours, unable to even blink. My breathing was laboured because my chest couldn't rise against the force of the clay. I was left alone with my thoughts and the few shadows that darted in front of me.

A memory from grade seven played out in my head. A bell rang. I was pulling my books out of my locker as students swarmed into classrooms all around me. Out of nowhere, Kyle pushed me into the narrow locker and slammed the door. I heard the lock click shut. My body was crunched up, the feeling of pins and needles pricking my arms and legs.

I banged the locker and screamed for help but soon gave up. Through the vent slots, I could hear other students walk by, only caring enough to laugh at my crying. After what felt like an hour, bolt cutters snapped through the metal lock. The door opened and there was Javier, the custodian, and next to him stood Harper. She was so angry I had to spend the next week pleading with her not to murder Kyle.

My mind drifted even further back to grade three. Because my home life was affecting my behaviour at school, they put me into a remedial class. It was a terrible feeling, made worse by my dad's disappointment in me, but every day I would find a note from Harper waiting for me on my desk. It was usually a joke or a memory of something we had done, her way of letting me know that things would be okay. She never missed a day. Now, I wanted to help her. I needed to.

I heard something approach me. My breathing quickened and my stomach dropped. I thought it was

Cerberus ready to unveil another level of horror in this garden. Instead, I felt something picking at the clay, chipping small pieces off my face. It didn't stop until my face was uncovered. I must have blinked a hundred times trying to get my eyes to focus. When they finally did, I was looking at the young woman I had seen leaving Pazuzu's house earlier. She stood in front of me, arms crossed, a serious look on her face.

"It's possessed clay and will re-form, so answer my questions quickly and honestly," she said. "Who are you?"

"Sam Sullinger. I've been in Hell for like half a day and it's really not going well."

"Ya don't say," she said.

More wet clay emerged from the ground, crawling over the set clay, moving toward my head.

"Where are you from?" she asked.

I searched for the right word. "Berdym."

She took a few steps toward me. Her expression became more severe.

"Where exactly are you from?"

"Earth! Canada! Toronto!" I said, hoping one of these would satisfy her. She smirked. It seemed those names had meaning to her.

"Please get me out of here!" I said.

"Who brought you to Hell?"

The clay was sliding up my shoulders. I was having trouble breathing, and my moment of relief was about to end.

"No one. I came on my own."

"Do you have a way to get home?"

"Yes! The same way I got here."

She moved right up to my face. This might have been the worst time to notice, but she smelled amazing.

The clay was crawling up my neck, almost reaching my chin.

"Listen to me. I will get you out of here, but only if you show me how you plan on getting home. If you lie to me, I'll kill you," she said.

My chin was now covered, making it hard to move my jaw and speak clearly.

"Get me to Belphegor and I'll give you anything you want."

"Belphegor?" she said, looking both confused and annoyed. "You really trying to make a deal right now?"

She was right, but I had to stay focused on finding Harper. Clay hardened around my head and I was once again trapped. To make matters worse, I had no idea if this stranger was actually going to help me. I prayed that I had said enough to convince her.

Minutes that felt like hours ticked by. I had no choice but to accept the fact that she had left me here to die.

My train of thought was broken by a grunt and a hard knock at the back of my head. Large chunks of clay were being pulled away from my shoulders and back. Next, she used her hands and an arrow tip to hack away the clay on my legs. As soon as my hands were released, I cleared the clay from my face. Finally, I was completely free. Only small pieces clung to my clothes.

I studied her as she picked up her satchel and crossbow.

"Thanks," I said.

"We need to get out of here," she said.

"Wait. I was brought here with someone else."

"Leave 'em."

"No, I can't."

She ignored me and walked away. I hustled to stay close to her. Something about her made me feel safer.

"What's your name?" I asked.

"Shut up," she said.

Beleth was deathly quiet. I must have been in the clay for hours, because it was now nighttime, the whole village sound asleep. The nameless young woman and I slunk behind the huts, away from the light of the torches that lined the street. My anxiety spiked each time we had to cross the open area between two huts.

We walked into the woods, not stopping until we reached a horse tied to a post. She mounted it.

"Hop on. The saddle fits two."

"We have to find my fr—"

I was interrupted by the ringing of a bell. Hanbi demons carrying torches came out of their huts and marched toward the gallows. The world had gone dark, but Beleth was now visible in the light of fire.

The Hanbi parted into two lines, creating a path that led to the gallows. They all had the same distinctive white skin, dark contours, and red eyes of their leader, Pazuzu.

"What are they doing?" I asked, but was met with a harsh *shush*.

At the far end of the path, Cerberus appeared with Thorlton in front of him. He marched Thorlton through the line of Hanbi, who hissed and spat at him. Some even kicked dirt in his face. Thorlton's body quivered, and his lower lip trembled. His pleas for his life were drowned out by the shouts and jeers of the crowd. Watching him made my eyes prick with tears.

"We have to help him," I said.

"Are you crazy?" she said.

"I can't leave him."

She ran her hand through her hair with frustration. But she seemed to be at least considering my position.

Cerberus walked Thorlton onto the platform under the gallows, above the crowd. There Thorlton stood before all the inhabitants of Beleth, who had closed the path and were now huddled together in front of the gallows.

There was no way I was going to let Thorlton die, but I had no chance of saving him without her help.

"I can't leave him," I said.

"The Hanbi and the Incubi have hated each other for a long time. You don't want to get involved."

"Please," I pleaded.

"Can't you just be happy that your friend is a useful distraction while we escape?" she whispered. "And keep your voice down." A good suggestion, since we were only partly hidden by the cover of the woods.

"Well, I'm going to help him. And if anything happens to me, you're out of luck. I might even tell them that you were the one who freed me."

She sat still in the saddle, thinking, her expression hard. One chance to close the deal.

"If you help him, I'll do whatever it takes to get you what you want."

"Get on," she said through gritted teeth.

It took me a few tries, but I eventually mounted the horse. I wrapped my arms around her waist, which she clearly didn't appreciate. She clicked her heels. The horse began to trot around the huts.

On the platform, Thorlton was waddling back and forth, wringing his hands. His sweat mixed with tears as Cerberus tested a noose. The crowd ominously chanted "Alchem, Alchem."

We stopped before we reached the back of the crowd. We watched Cerberus step to the edge of the platform and slide the noose over Thorlton's head and down to his neck.

Cerberus paused. The young woman seized the opportunity by rapping her heels hard and flicking her wrists, sending the horse into a fierce gallop. When we were about halfway to the gallows, the crowd turned toward us, gasping in shock.

She lifted off the saddle, pulled out her crossbow, and, with perfect coordination, fired an arrow over the crowd and into Cerberus's shoulder, knocking him off the platform. She lowered herself back into the saddle.

The Hanbi jumped to the side. Most ran off, some getting trampled.

I was awestruck. If it had been me holding the reins, I could never have pulled that off.

The horse leaped onto the platform.

"Sam. Sam. Sam," Thorlton said.

The young woman pulled him onto her lap.

A shriek pierced the air. All three of us turned our heads and saw a brutal-looking creature crawling along the roof of Pazuzu's house. He had long yellow fangs and sharp talons that cracked the stone as he crawled. His eyes bled. The sight of him made me shudder.

"Who's that?" I asked.

"That's Pazuzu," she replied.

We were so distracted by Pazuzu that we didn't notice the crowd returning.

"Okay, time to go," the young woman said.

She tapped her heels and the horse ran the length of the platform, jumped off and carried us into the woods. I watched the torches flicker until we were so far away that the light could no longer reach us.

HOLLINSHEAD

My parents once dragged my siblings and me on a road trip. We drove from Toronto to the east coast of Canada, hopped on a ferry to Maine, and then drove to Cape Cod and finally to Boston. Every place was so different, even though they weren't very far apart. The more we travelled, the more I learned that the world was a big place, more than just the street I lived on or the school I went to every weekday. That's why I loved Cloaked Atlas. It might have been just a poorly lit room above a dim sum restaurant, but it let me experience other times and places, other lives that were better than my own.

I was now feeling the same sense of discovery I'd felt on that road trip. The big difference was that Hell wasn't a scenic, calm land, and I wasn't protected from the outside world by a station wagon filled with my annoying siblings and the sound of Neil Diamond songs. I wasn't close to my family, sure, but being in a new world made me miss them. No matter how cold my dad was to me, I still had warm memories of my mom hugging me before I left for school and of Aaron and me playing video games. I tried not to think of the morning after I left, but I kept imagining my parents calling my name from the bottom of the stairs. When I didn't answer, they would assume I had spent the night at Harper's or at Cloaked Atlas. Only when they called my name again the next day would they realize their son was gone.

The horse trotted on the soft ground through the maze of thick tree trunks. Brown and black leaves obstructed most of my view of the sky, but I could see just enough to notice that it had mellowed into a lighter shade, now closer to orange than red.

Hell's dawn.

I had asked the young woman for her name three times, but each time she ignored me. She hadn't said much since Beleth. I told her about my backpack and gave her a vague description of the gully behind the boulder, and we headed back toward Mara.

"So that was Beleth? I always pictured it as being bigger," I said.

"Mmm hmm," she said, sounding disinterested.

"The Hanbi, though, those guys are pretty gross," I said.

"Do you have an off switch?"

"So, what's your name?" I asked again, ignoring her coldness.

"If I tell you will you stop talking?"

"Forever," I said.

"Hollinshead," she replied.

"Hollinshead? Sounds Dutch."

I could only see the back of her head, but I still felt her disapproval. I think she had rolled her eyes a dozen times since we met.

"So, where ya from?" I asked her, as if she were from a different school and we had bumped into each other at the skate park under the Gardiner Expressway.

"You talk too much," she said.

"Aren't you curious why I'm going to Belphegor? Or why I'm even here?"

"Not really," she said sharply. "You get one question."

"Three."

"One."

"Two, and I'll give you one veto," I said.

"Fine. Go."

Success! Now I had to make the most of this opportunity.

"So, you're like human?"

"Yup," she replied.

"Why are you in Hell?"

"Veto."

"Okay, fine. Why were you coming out of Pazuzu's?"

"He's my boyfriend and we got in a really big fight about prom," she said. Full points for her deadpan delivery.

She pointed up ahead to a large boulder. "Is that it?"

"Yeah. Yeah," Thorlton said.

The horse picked up speed. When we got to the boulder, I jumped off and ran to the gully, where I was thrilled to find the pile of twigs and leaves intact. I brushed them away and found my backpack lying there innocently. I was hit with a wave of relief. The box wasn't just the only way I had to solicit Hollinshead's help. It was also my only way home.

I took the box out of my backpack, but before handing it to her I said, "It's one of Alchem's Gifts, right?"

"Looks like it," she said.

"So you'll take me to Belphegor and I'll show you how it works?"

"That's our deal," Hollinshead said.

She smiled as she placed the box in her satchel.

"Careful with it. It's our only way home," I said.

I was starting to feel as if I actually had a small shot at finding Harper. Hollinshead seemed motivated enough to get me to Belphegor, but I was still worried about how I was going to find Stolas.

"It's far, so we'll have to stop along the way," she said.

We continued on horseback through the copse of trees heavy with leaves and nuts. It was quiet except for the clopping of the horse's hooves and the murmur of a waterfall gently feeding a babbling brook. The peacefulness cleared my mind. It was hard having a lot of demons try to kill you or turn you into a garden gnome. It was even harder missing your best friend and not knowing if you were too late to save her.

All I could do now was think of Harper, try not to annoy Hollinshead, and enjoy the calm before Belphegor.

RAGEWICK

After a couple of hours, we reached a border of trees that separated the woods from a rusty town. Held inside a fence made of pikes was a sea of roofs, their ridged design and different heights making them look like tin waves.

As we got closer, the horse slowed and tensed. Incessant screaming and cackling washed over us from the town. The horse let out a squealing neigh, roused by a bell that was ringing over the noise. I have to admit, being a city boy and all, the noise energized me, especially after the quiet of the woods.

The gates slowly opened, and we entered a town that seemed to reflect the grime and collective despair of its inhabitants.

"Don't say a word," Hollinshead said.

Two heavy-set demons, their long robes dragging in the mud, closed the gates behind us. One approached the horse as it slowed to a trot. Hollinshead reached into her pocket and flashed him a piece of paper.

"Two slaves for the auction," she said. He nodded and handed her a gold pin before walking away.

She handed me the pin and paper. "Put this on your shirt."

Hollinshead dismounted first and tied the horse to a post. I helped Thorlton down. He shuffled under the horse to shield himself from the onslaught of activity. I bet Mara never got this busy.

"Stay close," Hollinshead said.

We moved to obey her. To onlookers, I must have looked like a bewildered tourist, charmed by the sights and sounds of an unfamiliar city. The town was cramped, suffocating from the constant rush of demons and creatures struggling through the muck. Wagons and carts navigated the main road, which was lined with the empty, outstretched hands of beggars and the upturned hats of buskers covered head to toe in silver glitter. Across the street, demons sat in leather chairs, getting their shoes shined by creatures smaller than Thorlton. Shopkeepers and artisans leaned in the doorways along a block of businesses with finger-smudged windows and peeling wood: North & Sons Prospectors Co., Cure-Alls Apothecary, Malachi Bertree's General Store, and Zepp's Brewers, to name a few. Through a window, a soot-covered blacksmith, anvil between his legs, pounded glowing yellow iron with a mallet.

The streets were filled with demons yelling at their horses or stumbling around. Drunks emptied their stomachs of liquor and meat in the alleys. Ash dropped from the hot tips of cigarettes onto the dirt road defaced by footprints. In front of some barrels, a musician in a floppy hat strummed a lute and sang out of key. Next to him was an accordionist whose playing sounded like he was squeezing a wheezy child who had swallowed a horn.

Thorlton and I followed Hollinshead through the street. She knew this town.

"Where are we?" I asked, doing my best to keep up with her as passing demons knocked me in the shoulder.

"Ragewick," she replied.

Ragewick. Home of the Arkavelles. Stolas's home.

Just as the land bridge in the Bering Strait had allowed humans to cross from Asia to North America during the ice age, a lost explorer's discovery of the Nybbas Strait led demons to Hell's shore. Eventually, the Arkavelles arrived and forcefully took the northern river town of Ragewick. They carved out their own little world of slaves, thieves, drunks, and debauchery, and had lived that way ever since.

The skin of most Arkavelles looked like that of burn victims, tight and scarred. They liked extravagant facial hair: moustaches that touched sideburns and thick beards. It was clear from how they carried themselves that they were demons with cold dispositions and harsh temperaments. I would have crossed the street to avoid them, but they were on both sides of the street.

"I'm in a rush, okay?" I said, loud enough so that Hollinshead could hear me over the street noise.

"It's all about romance with you Berdymians," she said.

Hollinshead entered a doorway, cutting off a demon with tufts of wild hair. I snuck a look at the wooden sign as we followed her inside. It read "Lady Baxter's Inn."

A pianist was playing a tune so melancholy that it

sounded like every note was causing the piano great pain. Empty mugs sat on a polished wooden bar. Flowery wallpaper and purple-curtained windows made this place a warm respite from the outside world. Still, it was the kind of place where you ate in silence and minded your own business.

The stubby critter-like waitress dropped three full mugs on the table. Hollinshead handed her a few reodes, which she shoved into her apron pocket. Hollinshead didn't seem to mind footing our bill, which was good because I was broke.

"Woom at the end of the hall," the waitress said in a squeaky voice, obviously having trouble with her *r* sounds. "Would you like the special?"

Hollinshead nodded, and the waitress shuffled off.

"Room?" I asked.

"The horse needs to rest," Hollinshead said. "He's carrying extra weight."

I noticed that she had trouble looking me in the eyes, as if she didn't want to acknowledge my existence. I could now see her high cheekbones and speckled green eyes. She was built like a runner — everything about her was confident. It was easy to imagine her racing down Spadina Avenue after a streetcar.

She leaned close to me, her face so intense it made me nervous. "Don't take that thing off," she said, referring to the piece of paper hanging from my shirt.

"What is it?"

"A town pass. It's pretty much the only thing that will stop an Arkavelle from eating you." She paused. "I'm kidding."

I exhaled.

"But seriously, keep it on or they'll kill you or sell you or something."

I had no clue how to respond to that, so I just stared at the table.

"Thorlton?" Thorlton said, a finger pointed at his chest.

"You're fine. They don't care about your kind," she said. He seemed happy with her response.

It wasn't lost on me that she had given me the town pass for protection, opening herself up to danger. In fairness, though, I needed it a lot more than she did.

"I can't believe I'm in Ragewick," I said. "I mean, the bell tower down the street is where Stolas joined the Architects."

"Neat," she replied half-heartedly. "But try to act less like a tourist."

"You come here a lot?" I asked.

Every question felt like trespassing. She threw back her drink. Taking her cue, I leaned back and took a sip from my mug. It was warm and bitter, with an acidic aftertaste.

"Oh my god, what is this?"

"It's good. No? Perry cider," Thorlton said. He chugged his, spilling most onto his face and chest.

The waitress stared at me angrily, not appreciating my comment about her drink, before disappearing into the kitchen.

The sounds of revelry drifted in from the street as the inn door opened and closed. As the dinner rush started, Arkavelles filled the tables and lined the bar. Ragewick seemed about as open to outsiders as Beleth was, and that wasn't a good thing.

Hollinshead caught me scanning the bar.

"Easy with the staring, buddy," she said, and then tilted her head toward a table of grey-skinned demons with severe expressions. "Most Arkavelles won't hesitate to kill someone for looking at them wrong."

I nodded and shifted my body so that I was facing only her. I was hyperaware that anything I did could be the last thing I would ever do.

"All right, so why Belphegor?" she asked.

I was shocked that she was showing an interest. It felt kind of nice.

"My best friend, Harper, was taken, and the answer for saving her is in Belphegor," I said. Even the mention of Harper's name or the thought of that night made my eyes sting.

"And what answer is that?"

"A demon named Stolas. Ever heard of him?"

"Nope," she said. "But I got news for you: no one comes to Hell just for a friend."

Her assurance called my bluff. I didn't know what to say. Even in the privacy of my mind, describing my love for Harper was hard. It was an instinct more than anything. I had thought about her every day since kindergarten.

Hollinshead stared, concentrating on my face like a laser beam, waiting for an explanation.

"She's the only person who's really ever mattered to me. She's sweet and smart and funny and beautiful," I said.

Hollinshead awkwardly looked away. Thorlton reacted differently, putting his hand on mine.

"That's a nice list. I also have a list." She took a deep breath. "Here are just some of the ways that someone like you will die in Hell. You can be eaten by a Wanderer, killed by a Banshee, beaten to a pulp by an Arkavelle, burned at the stake by a Jinn — because they love burning Berdymians. There's the Kappa monster, grey boil fever, the Volacs, the Celebration of Vickory —"

"A celebration sounds nice," I said.

"It is, yet somehow hundreds still die." Her sense of ease was concerning. "It's a big world, and every inch of it will find a clever way to end your life."

I sat in stunned silence. Her eyes slowly softened until finally, she seemed to take pity on me.

"I'll help you find this Stolas guy, but then we're done," she said. By the look on her face, she was immediately annoyed with her own generosity. I, on the other hand, wanted to celebrate, but this really wasn't the place.

The waitress brought out a silver platter filled with sausages bursting at both ends and the small wings of some creature, burned to a crisp. A yellow herb garnished the meal. Hollinshead and Thorlton wasted no time digging in. I picked up a wing and dangled it in front of me.

"This is definitely not chicken." I tossed it back on the platter. Thorlton picked it up and shoved it in my face.

"Eat, Sam. Eat."

The only way to get him to stop was to start eating. I took a tiny bite. I promise you, it didn't taste like chicken.

With full stomachs, we headed upstairs and down a long hallway. We opened the door to our room to find a sad bed and a lantern. At least it was an upgrade from Pazuzu's garden.

"You two can sleep on the floor," Hollinshead said.

She tossed her satchel on the bed and pulled off her boots. I studied her some more. The same piece of hair constantly fell in front of her face, and there were a few tiny cuts around her neck. She was athletic and didn't look a bit tired, whereas my body felt bashed and beaten. It was her eyes, though, that captivated me, hardened and secretive, hinting at the wheels turning behind them.

I sat on the floor, leaning against the bedpost, my mind wandering to the garden where, not long ago, I'd been a prisoner. Even a flicker of those thoughts made me anxious.

I noticed that what I'd first thought was a tattoo on the inside of Hollinshead's wrist was actually scar tissue. A symbol of a scythe was burned into her skin. She caught me staring and pulled down her sleeve to cover the mark. I looked away before I offended her even more.

By the door, Thorlton wiggled out of his pants.

"Why don't we make this a pants sort of night?" Hollinshead said, and he begrudgingly pulled them back on. She got into the bed and pulled the thin sheet on top of her. She turned the lantern's knob and the room went dark.

I lay down on a sheet on the floor. The muted sounds of the busy tavern floated through the floorboards. I kept thinking of Harper. Thorlton snuggled up in front of me, making it worse.

In a desperate attempt to find comfort, my mind transformed the room into my bedroom at Cloaked Atlas. The walls turned blue and shelves appeared that held framed photos of me and Harper together. My desk took shape, dressed with a laptop and a stack of books. But in an instant, it was all gone. Plagued by worry, I returned to the coldness of my reality. What were my parents going through right now? If they hadn't figured out I was missing yet, they would very soon, and then I didn't know what would happen. Would my dad care? Would he come to Hell in search of me? My uncle's heart must have broken when he read my letter.

All I could think about was giving Harper that necklace and then watching her being dragged through the shop. That look on her face refused to leave me.

I couldn't take it anymore, so I left the room. I walked down a flight of stairs that led out of the building and found myself back out on the street, which was now quiet. A few buskers had stuck around, counting their haul and wiping off makeup. The beggars had left, most likely as poor as when they'd arrived. Everyone who walked by me glanced at the pass on my shirt.

Earlier, the musk of a hundred horses must have camouflaged the scent of urine, because now that was all I could smell. Making matters worse, a waterfall of urine fell from a tipped chamber pot held out of a window above. Some splashed on my shoes.

The bell tower loomed in the distance, its sharp point puncturing the red sky. In its belfry, Stolas had first met with the Architects, a cabal devoted to ending the reign of Emperor Belphegor.

I headed toward the tower, the mud making my shoes wet and heavy. On the other side of dirty windows, blurry silhouettes fought, drank, laughed, and yelled.

The mud ended once I arrived at the bell tower. In front of me was a doorway and stairs. I'm not sure why, but it felt safe to enter.

From the stairwell, I could see right up to the belfry, where the bell rested, silent. When I reached the top platform, awe overtook my fear. As I stood on the ledge, the view made me realize that my search was impossible. The land was bigger than my imagination.

Beautiful ivory mountains stood in a string, linked together by deep hammocks of valleys. Villages and towns crept up to the edges of undisturbed woods. A river curved through trees, connecting with other rivers that then parted again to wind on their own separate journeys. Why couldn't Hell just be a lake of fire or something? It would be easy to dredge a lake.

Someone cleared their throat in the far corner of the platform. I looked over and saw the lute player I'd seen in the street earlier. He was sitting on the ledge, working some dirt out from under his fingernail. His floppy hat rested on the floor next to him, allowing me to see his long nose and white hair. Lines marred his face.

"New to Ragewick, I see. The look on your face gives you away. Good thing you have a town pass," he said, firing off words like a machine gun. "Berdymian, huh?"

I was too nervous to respond.

"Be careful around here. Berdymians aren't held in very high regard."

Scared that he was charming me into an attack, I thought about my knife, which was still in my backpack. I should have taken it out before I left to wander this strange, dangerous town. His next move was to tell me that his name was Boyer. He picked up his lute and began tuning it.

"I sleep up here when I don't make enough money to please that harpy Lady Baxter," he said, and then waved the thought away as if it annoyed him. "So, what brings you to Ragewick?"

"I'm on my way to Belphegor."

"The falling jewel of Hell. And what awaits you there? A fine redheaded Jinn, I hope."

"Someone named Stolas. He's in one of the mines," I said as I took a seat on the floor.

He leaned forward curiously, his eyes showing doubt.

"Well, I'll be sure to write a mournful song for you when you are killed by a Banshee," he said.

He slunk from the ledge to the ground and let out a big yawn.

"Is it true that you can control a Banshee by whispering in their ear?" I asked, recalling Camio, a demon who formed the Banshees into his own army as he fought Emperor Belphegor for control of the Gwyn River. He lost, and the Banshees were returned to their role as guardians of the mines.

"So the legend goes. If you can capture one, speak the name of a prisoner into their ear and they'll do the rest," he said, knitting his eyebrows, apparently sorting some thoughts. "Or maybe it's just folklore, since no one has ever wanted to break someone out of the mines." He placed his hat on his head, tilting it forward to cover his eyes, and wished me luck.

As I walked back toward the inn, a raspy voice yelled, "Sam. Sam."

Thorlton was nervously poking his head into every alley, looking for me, getting kicked away by anyone he got too close to. As soon as he spotted me, he ran and wrapped his arms around my waist.

"Sam. Sam. You were gone."

I calmed him down, and we walked back to the inn and entered through the side door. We crept up the stairs and lay down next to the bed where Hollinshead slept.

Even though I was cuddling with a little demon, I felt very alone.

THE CITY OF BELPHEGOR

We awoke early and left Lady Baxter's right away.
Hollinshead told us to stay quiet as we
approached the gates on horseback. The same
demon who had given us the pass the day before walked
up to the horse. He held on to the reins to make sure we
stayed put.

"You declared them as slaves upon entry."

"Yeah, no one wanted them," Hollinshead replied,
then turned to look at us. "Too small and too stupid."

The demon looked at Thorlton and me and laughed.
He let go of the reins.

We left Ragewick, hopefully for good. I thought
about my conversation with Boyer, which didn't exactly
fill me with confidence. What would I find in Belphegor?
Were the stories true? More importantly, who — or what
— was waiting for me in the mines?

"The gold pin and the pass," Hollinshead said, reaching her hand back. I gave her the items and she put them
in her pocket.

The horse took us along a straight path in the woods. Every so often, a wagon or carriage would roll by in the opposite direction. At most, Hollinshead would give it a nod. I got the impression that she liked to keep to herself.

Thorlton, on the other hand, liked to talk. He was enjoying the company, and it felt as if he, too, was experiencing Hell for the first time.

I was sore from sitting on the horse for so long, and my muscles still ached from the flight to Beleth and then the clay. During the last leg of our journey in the forest, I noticed through the trees that murky grey smoke was strangling the normally red sky.

We emerged into a vast green field. On the other side I could see a place much different from both Mara and Ragewick. In fact, it made both of them look like quaint hamlets. I held my breath as I admired its greatness.

This was a city. This was Belphegor.

Named after the emperor who commissioned its construction, Belphegor roared with energy. It was as if the journey from Ragewick to Belphegor had taken a hundred years and I was now in the future, even if this future was closer to Victorian England than present day Toronto. Still, it was impressive.

There was no gate or guard. We simply rode in and tied the horse to a metal post. Iron-shod wheels and hooves clacked along cobbled roads that shone like marble, gilded carriages pulled by strong stallions passed each other, and every street was numbered. I stood at the corner of 4th and 11th. Blocks of shops and other buildings were hugged by outer rings of castles, which made the huts of rural Beleth look like, well, huts. The buildings here weren't just simple clapboard either. They were stone, terracotta, and perfect red brick. It was architecture designed with great care. In Ragewick, the streets were stuffed so tightly, with no thought given to space or comfort. You couldn't walk without brushing a shoulder or feeling a horse's hot breath. Belphegor, on the other hand, gave you room to breathe.

Evidence of my own world was everywhere. I tried not to gawk at the Berdymians who walked alongside demons or appeared behind half-curtained carriage windows. I didn't know if they were slaves or companions, and while Belphegor did feel safer than Ragewick and Beleth, I still wasn't going to ask.

Thorlton and I followed Hollinshead down the street, past a general store, a haberdashery, and a string of bodegas that sold everything from wine to books to pomades, or so the signs in the windows claimed.

I stopped in front of a shop with a green awning that read "Cipher Office." Through the window, I could see imps stuffing letters into envelopes and then sealing the envelopes with wax. These pink-bodied, winged demons were ciphers — a cross between a postal worker and a carrier pigeon — whose job it was to deliver messages all over Hell. When I was seven, I told my uncle that I wanted to be a cipher. Being the guy that he was, he built me wings and a body out of papier mâché, painted it all pink, and had me deliver letters to the other businesses along Spadina. He told me they were important communiqués, but really they were just greeting cards.

"Keep moving. I don't wanna drag this out," Hollinshead said.

We continued through the rambling city. It was bustling, yet the atmosphere was polite and much more diverse than the other places I'd been to so far. The blend of refinement and demons was dizzying. I even caught a few smiles.

I recognized most of the races. Arkavelles, Krauss, Alpsecords, and Jinns had all congregated in this city. There were demons with grey skin, some with dark skin, and many whose skin was red or light green. Some had wings and others had tails; a few had neither. Horns were long and curled or filed to a sharp point. The clothing was eclectic: suits, tunics, elaborate dresses with low necklines and trains, frock coats, top hats, and ascots. There were no buskers or beggars. Music did fill the streets, though, coming from the open windows of the shops and castles.

We walked a long way to the edge of the city's sprawl, beyond the commercial area, then across a long stone bridge to an industrial outskirt. The factories emitted smells of chemicals and raw meat. Chimney stacks pushed out smoke, which settled into a nest above Belphegor. On the grounds of one factory, a line of sickly Berdymians, chained neck to neck, swung pickaxes, cracking the ground. They had a tolerance for gloom and hard labour, having been trained to only pay attention to the target of their pickaxe.

Hell was a world built on the backs of people. It was hard to see my own kind as worthless, to see myself that way. Even harder was trying not to imagine Harper sentenced to this fate. What was she going through right now?

"Keep walking," Hollinshead said, noticing that my attention had drifted.

Beyond the factories was a graveyard where patches of grass surrounded row upon row of grave markers. There were thousands of them, each inscribed with a name.

The great city was finally behind us. We stood before a stump of a hill. A carved doorframe opened into a passage that led down inside the hill. Thorlton shivered from fright, so I patted him on the head like I would a child.

The mines were a prison designed to encase enemies of the empire and the worst offenders in rock for all of eternity. There were no stays of execution or kindhearted governors calling wardens at the eleventh hour. Once your skin was melted off, your bones no longer belonged to you.

"So we just walk in?" I said nervously.

"Yup," Hollinshead replied. "The complex is made up of hundreds of mines and tunnels. It's too much area to cover. We'll need help."

"From a Banshee?"

"Well, aren't you an A student? They're dangerous, so we have to try to corner one and whisper Stolas's name." She tied her ponytail tighter, then loaded an arrow into her crossbow.

I gave her a long look. It sounded simple, but nothing was ever that simple.

"What do we do after we find him?"

"I don't know, man. I've done this as many times as you have. All I know is we have to get out of here before curfew."

"What curfew?"

"Notice how we walked right into the city? That's because it protects itself," Hollinshead said. She made an annoyed sound, clearly not appreciating having to explain things to me.

"From the Wanderers," I said.

"Bingo. The city descends once one is spotted. And we can't get caught after doing whatever it is we're about to do. And if we wait, then you're just making your friend wait." She emphasized the word *friend*, having already figured out how to twist the knife in my heart.

I wasn't going to proceed unarmed like I had in Ragewick. I removed the knife from backpack and placed it in the waistband of my pants. Hollinshead didn't say anything else before taking her first step toward the entrance. A gust of wind whistled through the opening. It sounded like a scream and caused my skin to pebble with gooseflesh. Maybe those should have been two big red flags, but it wouldn't have mattered. Nothing could have prepared me for what was about to happen.

Mounds and hills of sedimentary rock the colour of charcoal, flecked with red ash, stretched for miles in all directions. Among them were shallow pits of oil covered with blue and orange flames. As if following a fat trail of kerosene, lines of fire weaved up and down and around corners.

With every step we took into the mine, the stench grew stronger. I had never experienced such a smell before: death, skin, blood, and decay all under a constant heat lamp. It was disgusting. Thorlton, tongue hanging out the side of his mouth, looked close to fainting from the heat.

We hid behind a rocky mound. Above us, dozens of Banshees — ghostly female creatures with light-green skin and long white hair and dressed in black gowns — sailed through the air close to the ceiling. It was unsettling to watch them eerily float through one another. Their wailing echoed through the mine.

I took in the details of my surroundings. Skulls, spines, ribs, wings, and other bones were embedded in rock. It looked like an excavated ruin from an ancient civilization. I ran my fingers along a warm protruding bone, feeling every tiny bump.

Between the heat and the bones, I felt like there was a rock in my stomach. I bent over and dry heaved, bile rising in my throat. A Banshee heard me and stopped midair. She framed me in her crosshairs, let out a massive scream, and then jetted in my direction.

Terror gripped my throat, and my instincts, which were always to run and hide, kicked in. I sprinted up a slope only to trip and fall down the other side. I got up and found a crevice so narrow I had to turn sideways to fit.

The Banshee landed in a crouch, sending dirt into the air. She slowly approached my hiding spot, walking barefoot on the sharp, hard ground. I tried to push farther into the dark hole, but a wall stopped me from disappearing completely. I squeezed my eyes shut, my entire body tensing as I waited to be caught. The Banshee reached into the crevice, her cold fingers grazing my arm. But before she could clutch my shirt sleeve, Hollinshead dropped from the top of the slope, tackling her to the ground. They rolled a few times until the Banshee flipped Hollinshead on her back and began choking her. Hollinshead struggled for air, trying to pry the Banshee's hands from her throat. Thorlton appeared and bit the Banshee's arm, but she tossed him against a rock.

The look of desperation in Hollinshead's eyes told me that she would kill the Banshee to survive, but we needed her to help us find Stolas. There was also a good chance that killing one would alert the others.

The Banshee pursed her white lips close to Hollinshead and whispered into her ear. Almost immediately, Hollinshead's face turned white and blue veins pushed against her skin.

I slid out of the crevice and approached them. I lowered my mouth to the Banshee's ear, but before I could whisper Stolas's name, another one swooped down and grabbed my shoulders, lifting me off the ground.

I kicked and screamed as the Banshee pulled me higher into the air. Remembering the knife in the back of my pants, I pulled it from my waistband and stabbed it into her arm. She winced in pain and released me. I landed hard on the ground as she returned, dazed, to the ceiling.

The other Banshee was still on top of Hollinshead, whose face now looked decrepit. She was seconds from death. Thorlton rushed over and tried to pull the Banshee off by her leg. I ran over, lowered my mouth to her ear, and whispered "Stolas." The name worked like a spinning hypnosis wheel, entrancing her.

Her head lifted and her shoulders straightened. Her eyes turned a milky white as she let go of Hollinshead. The colour slowly returned to Hollinshead's face.

"Are you okay?" I asked her.

"I'll live," she said through a fit of coughing.

The Banshee stood up and said, "If it is he you seek, then follow me."

I mouthed a silent *yes* in celebration.

The Banshee escorted us through a network of tunnels that connected the different mines, running her hand along the rock wall, whispering the name of the owner of each bone. Whenever one of her kind noticed us from above, she would mutter something and they would continue on their way.

At the other end of the mine, the Banshee stopped and stared at the ground. Like an eerie hymn, she whispered Stolas's name over and over again.

"We got a hit," Hollinshead said. We ran to find the bones of a hand lodged in rock. The finger bones were bent, looking as if the last thing this hand had gripped was a baseball bat.

The Banshee raised her arms, causing the rock all around us to shift, making it tough to keep our balance. The wind built to a mini-tornado, and its force unearthed the hand from the rock's grasp.

"This is really messed up," I said.

"Leaving! Sam! Leaving!" Thorlton said as the Banshee continued walking between the mounds.

After a few minutes, she was at it again, unleashing her power to command the mine. More bones — femurs, hips, and spines — were removed from rock. An almost complete skeleton hovered above our heads.

We entered a cave shrouded in darkness, blindly following the Banshee's glow. Bones crunched under every step and my elbows scraped the walls. As we reached the end of the cave, her light cut through the dark, revealing a grotesque display of demon skulls before us.

The Banshee stared at one skull in the middle as she repeated "Stolas" under her breath. I moved closer to inspect it. The skull was smooth, with a ridged forehead and a straight set of brown-tinted teeth. I had only ever seen a skull on TV. Seeing one in person, it was hard to imagine it had ever been under skin.

Magically, the rock loosened and dirt fell out of the eye sockets and nasal cavity. The skull shot out of the wall and rocketed between us to join the other bones outside the cave.

"I think that's everything," I said, feeling some relief that maybe we were nearing the end. I was craving fresh air.

The Banshee smiled at me and walked out of the cave. We trailed her to an open space in the centre of the mine. The bones fell to the ground. Hollinshead put whatever she could into her satchel, and I filled my backpack with the rest. Here I was stuffing a demon's bones into my school backpack, when just a few days earlier my parents were yelling at me for playing a violent video game on the family computer.

The Banshee looked drained of energy as she escorted us to the exit.

"You have broken the law of the emperor. We will come for the bones," she said before flying off to join the others.

Once outside, I gulped the air like cold water. I was surprisingly calm as we walked toward the city and even felt some relief when my feet touched cobblestone.

"We can't be spotted. What we just did is considered treason," Hollinshead said. Heeding her warning, we kept to alleys and side streets on our way back to our horse.

"I thought that went pretty well," I said.

My words were a taunt that the city took exception to. As soon as they were out of my mouth, I felt something under the soles of my shoes. The first few trembles were faint. The next ones felt seismic, like the start of an earthquake.

Note to all future Sams who will bone-headedly travel to Hell to save the love of their life: Nothing is ever easy. Nothing.

"What was that?" I said, startled by what I had just felt. What all of Belphegor had just felt. Hollinshead might have just fought a Banshee, but in that moment, she looked as if she had seen a ghost. I looked around me, feeling a sense of shock I couldn't describe.

"Curfew. Hurry!" she shouted.

My heart and stomach collided. We picked up the pace as the road broke free of the sidewalk. The cobblestones lifted, releasing the sand that was holding them together. A chainsaw-like roar filled the air as shops and homes moved with the sinking ground.

The voice in my head repeated the words it had said when I arrived in Mara: *This is real. This is real. This isn't a dream.*

The city was slowly sinking, a curtain of silt falling from the ground it was separating from. As it sank, a vast wall that surrounded the city was revealed. The wall was pocked with dirt cubbyholes. It was a machine, but instead of being powered by electricity, it was powered by the effort of thousands of tiny demons standing in the cubbyholes, each controlling a set of pulleys that turned hidden wheels. They moved in concert, pulling and releasing the ropes above and below them. Each of their actions moved Belphegor a little farther away from the surface world.

The sour taste of panic rose in my throat. I was witnessing the emperor's vision come to life. Actually, I was in the middle of its craziness. I fully expected the streets to be filled with hysteria and everyone to be freaking out, but they weren't. Most were calmly entering buildings and shops for protection. They were treating the city's sinking as if it were nothing more than a bad storm, whereas I felt like a step in any direction would be my last.

Hollinshead whipped me around by my arm. Her eyes radiated intensity.

"I get that this is weird for you, but we need to get out of here."

"Okay," I said, but so quietly that there was no way she could hear me over all the banging and crashing. Her stare intensified.

"If we get caught, it's over. There's no hiding. There's no waiting it out. There's no Harper," she said, her hand on my shoulder.

I nodded, too scared to speak. We ran through the city trying to find our way back to the horse. We cut between two buildings, rounded one corner and then another until we were stopped, staring at a dead end made of bricks.

"We should have gone left!" I said.

"We did go left. Should have gone right." Hollinshead's breath quickened as she scanned the tops of buildings looking for a clue to guide us. At her urging, we left the alley and ran across the street and into another alley, where we found ourselves staring at three different but frustratingly identical paths, not knowing which was the right one. Every second that ticked by reduced our chance for escape.

"Look!" Hollinshead said, pointing toward the middle path. Her keen eye had spotted the green awning of the ciphers' office. Sprinting down the now empty road, we finally arrived at our horse, the only one left, who was fearfully stomping its hooves.

Hollinshead hopped on first, then pulled Thorlton onto her lap. Once again, it took me a few tries to get up. The first row of wall demons was fully uncovered. The city was sinking faster now. The sky was running away from us.

The wind broke against my face as we rode full speed through the deserted city, up the main street that was sinking lower with every pull from the demons. Tightening my arms around Hollinshead was the only thing I could do to keep myself from flying off.

"We can't make it," I said, fixated on the break in the land and the jump to safety that was becoming bigger by the moment. Hollinshead was like a determined jockey racing for the finish line.

Thorlton looked at me with the same expression he'd worn when he was being marched to the gallows. He moved his hand around, and for a second I thought he was making the sign of the cross, but then he shoved his whole hand into his mouth.

As we got closer to the wall, Hollinshead lifted her wrists and flicked the reins as hard as she could. The horse bent his front legs and tucked them under his body as he made a tremendous leap. But it was no use. The whole plan was one big miscalculation. The horse's head hit the wall between two demons mid-pull, well below the top. A bone cracked, followed by the horse's scream. As we fell, I reached over Hollinshead and was able to grab on to the ledge of one of the cubbyholes. Hollinshead yelled in pain as her hands grasped another ledge a few rows down. Thorlton held on to the waist of my pants, pulling them off my hip.

The horse desperately tried to right itself but was too frantic. He landed on the city street, between the jigsaw of buildings.

I got a better look at the demons whose efforts had hidden Belphegor from the rest of the world. They were stocky and muscular, with glassy eyes and severe under-bites. They fit perfectly in their dirt homes surrounded by ropes. Those near us craned their heads to get a look at the three of us hanging from the wall, sneering and greeting our presence with a chorus of grunts.

My hands turned white from the effort of holding on. Thorlton climbed up my body, using his nails as picks. Luckily, because of his size, he could climb into one of the empty cubbyholes. He moved up the inside of the wall, the same way the wall demons did, and eventually reached land. Perched above us, he watched our struggle for safety.

Hollinshead swung her body out and grabbed hold of another ledge. Gracefully, she climbed to the top. There was no doubt that she was a great athlete.

I wasn't a great athlete, though, and to make matters worse, I had to contend with a heavy backpack full of bones. My stomach twisted into familiar knots.

The cubbyholes didn't line up perfectly, so the journey to the top wasn't a straight line. I had reached about three-quarters of the way up. Below, the horse was lying on its side, thick streams of blood rushing away from its head. One after another, the torches that lined the city streets were snuffed out, blanketing Belphegor in darkness. I stopped to watch even though Hollinshead and Thorlton kept yelling at me to climb.

The wall demons had ceased their work. The city settled. For a moment, it was calm. Then the peace and quiet were shattered by the screams of the wall demons, who weren't happy about me hanging around. A few who were close enough scratched at me.

"Now would be a good time to start climbing," Hollinshead yelled, the urgency in her voice carrying all the way down to me.

I pulled myself up to another ledge, my body so close to quitting. As I reached for the next ledge, I was yanked back by a sharp pull on my backpack. A snaggle-toothed demon was trying to rip me off the wall and wasn't going to stop until I was next to the horse. I let go with one hand and swatted at him, but he kept ducking and leaning away from me. Another demon reached out and grabbed my ankle, digging his claws in.

My dirt-coated fingers were slipping off the ledge. I was about to lose my grip when an arrow struck the demon in the back. He screeched, then released me before falling off the wall, eventually splattering on the ground far below.

I looked up and there was Hollinshead. She had climbed down and was hanging off a ledge, crossbow in hand. A demon was slumped over, dead, in the hole in front of her.

"You're not really good at stuff, are you?" she said.

The demon holding my ankle tightened his grip. I wrenched my leg as hard as I could. Once free, I kicked it in the face, knocking him off the wall.

Hollinshead climbed farther down, close enough that I could see the detail on the soles of her boots.

"Follow me," she said.

I followed her path, which she was clearing of demons as she climbed. Each time one reached for her, she grabbed them by the neck and launched them out of the hole. Some merely retreated into their holes out of fear. I would have feared her as well if she weren't on my side.

I pulled myself up and reached for another ledge. From there I moved over to my right to get in a better position, placing my feet in the hole below.

Harper's voice in my head urged me to keep going.

I made it to a higher row of cubbyholes, passing demons that hissed and clawed at me. I kept climbing, using each cubbyhole to secure my foot and my grip. Hollinshead moved up the wall until she was back on land.

Finally, I was close enough. Hollinshead and Thorlton pulled me the rest of the way by my arms and backpack. Once on solid ground and far above the city streets, I rolled onto my back and stared at the grey sky.

"I thought that was it. I thought I was going to die," I said, trying to catch my breath. After being underground in the sticky heat of the mines and then pressed against a dirt wall, the fresh air filling my lungs was refreshing, like cannonballing into a cool ocean.

I looked at Hollinshead, who was checking her satchel to make sure the bones were still there. She winked at me. I wanted to thank her, but that probably would have only annoyed her.

The three of us stood there, looming over a mighty city that now seemed small and insignificant.

"So that was Belphegor," I said.

"Yup. And we need to keep moving," Hollinshead said.

Thorlton licked his palm in agreement.

THE WANDERERS

"**M**ove faster," Hollinshead said for the tenth time.

I wanted to move more quickly, but fear glued my feet to the ground in this stretch of land between the City of Belphegor and the rest of civilization. I was terrified that every far-off sound was a creature stealthily approaching. This forest was home to the Wanderers. Most troubling was that we hadn't come across a single soul since escaping the city, not even a bird overhead. For good reason, I was sure.

After Belphegor was dethroned in Tybalt, he set sail in search of a new world. A villager who spotted his ship at sea claimed that the jackal-headed former prince arrived amid swirling winds and rain. His pets, the Calfi, were his only cargo. Locked away in the aft of the ship, the Calfi arrived hungry. When Stolas beheaded Belphegor, the Calfi fled to the wild. A writer later noted that the Calfi wandered the traumatized world. Thereafter, they became known as the Wanderers.

We made our way through pockets of bright-coloured wildflowers, twigs underfoot. I had to keep urging Thorlton to walk, as he wanted to stop and sniff everything. I even had to pull some glowing green mushrooms out of his mouth.

With every step, the bones rattled in my backpack, bringing back an image of the mines. I still couldn't believe we'd made it. I was starting to feel a little proud of myself.

We walked along a ridge of grassy hills. When we reached the crest, we saw what looked to me like an oasis. Between two groups of withered white birches stood a one-storey log cabin with a wooden gable roof. The smell reminded me of summers back home, where every morning the dew brought out the aroma of the plants, earth, and pavement.

"I think we've gone far enough," Hollinshead said. It was the first time she sounded unsure of anything, but I was too tired to question it.

In front of the cabin, a rust-coloured pump curved out of the ground. I pushed the heavy handle down a few times, and a stream of murky water poured out. After a few more pumps, the water cleared. We took turns shoving our faces under the cold water, washing away the salty taste of the mines.

I sat next to Thorlton on a flat rock. Hollinshead scouted the perimeter, then reached through the glass-less window to push open a set of shutters and peer inside the cabin. Finally, she inspected the trees for scratch marks. There were no signs of life, so it seemed safe to go in.

"We need rest and food. We also need to deal with our new travel companion," Hollinshead said.

The cabin was just one big room with a small bedroom to the side. The only items in the entire place were a rocking chair, a wooden table, and a large fireplace.

I poked my head into the bedroom. It was more like a big walk-in closet than a livable space. Hollinshead flopped down onto the chair. I dropped my backpack as Thorlton scurried back outside.

"What if he can't help you?" she asked, flicking her head toward the backpack.

"There's no going back now. He's all I got," I said.

"That's not true. You'll still have Thorlton." She laughed.

"Right. Thorlton."

I sat on the ground. I didn't know where this journey would take me next, so I told myself that it was okay to enjoy a short breather, to feel safe hidden within the forest.

"Let's check our haul," Hollinshead said.

She opened her satchel and placed the bones of two feet on the table. I pulled the zipper of my backpack and winced as I grabbed a leg bone and laid it above the foot. Bone by bone we built a skeleton: feet, legs, spine, ribs, arms, hands, and skull.

I marvelled at our creation, mainly at its weirdness. I was lost in thought when the door burst open. There stood Thorlton holding the ankle of some dead creature that looked sort of like a warthog. It was twice his size.

"Hungry? Sam? Hungry? Hollinshead? Hungry?"

The warthog-like thing, now minus an ear and some belly meat, was on the floor, a pile of twigs acting as a platter. Hollinshead had done her best to prepare and cook it. She had started the fire and then skewered the poor beast with a thick branch, balancing the ends of the stick atop piles of rocks that flanked the fire. The collecting of rocks was my official contribution.

We sat on the ground to enjoy our first meal since our dinner at Lady Baxter's the night before. As I bit into large chunks of meat, each piece melted in my mouth. I caught Hollinshead looking at me and I smiled at her, then realized I had a piece of animal skin stuck on my cheek. We all kept sneaking glances at the skeleton on the table.

"What's with the crossbow?" I asked with a full mouth, not caring about manners.

"Gets the job done. I'm not trying to impress anyone."

"I can respect that. Ya know, you never told me why you're in Hell," I said.

The look on her face told me that I had trespassed once again. "Let me ask you something," she replied, wiping her mouth on the inside of her arm. "Is Harper your girlfriend?"

"No, not exactly," I replied, not sure if that was the answer she wanted to hear.

"And why this Stolas guy?"

"He was a hero," I said. "I read all about him in *The Book of Stolas*."

She huffed as if I had said something stupid. "That's it? We did all that 'cause of some book? They're just stories, Sam. They don't mean anything."

"It's something, at least. I know he can help me," I said. "Now it's your turn to answer a question. Why were you coming out of Pazuzu's when I first saw you?"

She looked away from me. "He promised to help me get home if I did something for him."

"What did you have to do?"

Once again, Hollinshead, a master of stonewalling, closed herself off. She got up, walked to the table, and stood over the bones. She flicked the skull with her finger.

"Well, why don't we deal with Stolas, and then you can be on your way," I said, joining her at the table. "How does this work? Like, how do we actually bring him back to life?"

She shot me a curious look. "Beats me."

"Don't know. Thorlton don't know," Thorlton said, tapping his temple. He then dropped to his hands and knees and took a bite right out of our dinner's belly.

I leaned against the table, a horrible feeling rising inside of me.

"Nothing about resurrecting dead guys in one of your precious books?" Hollinshead asked.

Her snarky comment triggered my memory. "Wait a minute," I said, remembering *The Leper Monks' New Incantations* and what Raymond had said. I reached into my backpack and pulled it out. "The answer's got to be in here."

I paced as I leafed through the pages, not quite sure what I was looking for. Out of the corner of my eye, I could see Hollinshead, shoulder against the wall, shaking her head in disbelief. A small line formed between her eyebrows.

Then I saw it. Under the words *Ossa sunt in spiritus. Resurgent* was a black-and-white drawing of several winged demons standing over a shallow grave filled with bones. I flipped the page, then turned the book so that it faced Hollinshead and Thorlton.

"Look," I said, tapping my finger on the double spread, where more Latin words appeared above another drawing of the grave. The skeleton was clawing its way out.

"This is it. It has to be." I shoved the book in Hollinshead's face. Then I turned to an earlier page and saw an image of a skeleton with each limb splayed. I made sure that the bones on the table resembled the ones in the picture. I read the words, "*Cinis ex inferno, et corpus ad ortum,*" and stepped back, waiting for life to bloom before my eyes.

Nothing happened.

"Why didn't it work?" I said.

I placed the book next to Stolas's bones. Hollinshead patronized me with a pat on the shoulder, and Thorlton leaned his head on my leg, then, for some reason, licked my knee.

"What am I going to do now?"

A loud bang on the roof startled us, causing dirt and dust to fall to the floor. Another bang, and then another that was even louder. The window shutters clattered so hard that they fell off their hinges.

"Thorlton, where did you find our dinner?"

"Ummm … dead under tree," he said, wringing his hands.

"Why does that matter?" I asked Hollinshead.

"Because something else killed our dinner," she said, a tremble in her voice. Her eyes tracked the footsteps on the roof, an arrow now taut in her crossbow. "I thought we were far enough."

The sweetness in the air was replaced by an acrid smell. The cabin filled with the sound of clawed feet pushing through the brush outside. I remembered a drawing I had seen of the Wanderers in one of my uncle's books. They had sinewy bodies and spider-walked on their hands and feet. Their eyes were sewn shut, crust lining the amateur stitching. Their mouths were full of bloody teeth and sharp fangs, which I could already imagine ripping through my body. We desperately looked around, trying to figure out a plan.

"We need to hide," I said, my voice breaking with fear.

"Great idea. You go under the table and I'll sit really still in the chair," Hollinshead said. Thorlton laughed nervously.

"Fine! So what's the plan?"

"We fight."

"Okay, here's the thing. I don't know how to fight, have never been in a fight, and, well, I just don't care for the idea."

"How have you never been in a fight before?" Hollinshead said.

"I mean, I've been beaten up by a lot of people."

Hollinshead walked over to me and placed a hand on my shoulder. Her voice was steady despite the commotion outside. "Stay calm. And you might want to use your knife."

"To stab them?" I said.

"Yes, Sam, to stab them."

Through the window, we could see the Wanderers standing in a broken line, the skin around their mouths pulled tight. One of them bit into the neck of the inattentive one next to it, driving its fangs deep, releasing a gush of black blood.

I joined Hollinshead and Thorlton in a huddle.

"We're gonna die," I said. "What happens if I die in Hell?"

"Nothingness. Make choice. Very bad, Sam. The other place. Very bad," Thorlton said. He licked his armpit.

"Listen to me. They're blind, vicious, and easily distracted," Hollinshead said.

"I don't know what to do with that," I said.

A Wanderer snarled at us through the window. Hollinshead shot an arrow through its eye and it fell to the ground. She loaded another arrow.

The banging on the roof grew louder. The wood was being ripped apart. It collapsed and two Wanderers came crashing inside, showering the room with broken planks. They lifted their bodies until they were on all fours and searched for the scent of prey.

I picked Hollinshead's satchel off the floor and wrapped its strap around my hand. A Wanderer circled me like a jungle cat, then darted toward me. I whipped the satchel around, smacking it in the face. The creature fell on its side. My moment of pride was crushed when it started to get up.

Another Wanderer lunged at me, but Hollinshead intercepted it, tackling it to the floor. They rolled as she narrowly averted its snapping jaw, keeping it at bay with her forearm pressed against its jugular. Impulsively, I ran behind it and wrapped my arms around its neck. It arched its back, lifting me off my feet.

"Knife," Hollinshead said, her voice strained and breathless. Her arm was weakening against the determination of her attacker.

I let go of its neck and pulled my knife out of my waistband. As Hollinshead's arm dropped, the Wanderer opened its mouth. I steadied my hands, lifted the knife above my head, and slammed it into the Wanderer's back. Blood bubbled up before the creature toppled over.

As I helped her up, we exchanged a quick look of relief. But we had no time to catch our breath. Another four Wanderers dropped through the roof, more fought their way through the door, and the rest pushed through the window. They let out a sound that was a cross between a squeal and a growl. It stiffened my spine.

We stood in the middle of the cabin as creatures crawled around us. One of them ripped flesh from the stomach of another that was lying under the table. Another two joined in, eating its organs and entrails. In the opposite corner, my knife was sticking out of the back of the one I had just killed.

I tiptoed toward that corpse, focusing on my knife and hoping the others would remain distracted by feasting on their friend. I reached down and started to slowly pull out my knife. Before I had it all the way out, another Wanderer jumped me, pushing me onto my back, its claws on my shoulders. I reflexively covered my face with my arms for protection, giving the Wanderer the opportunity to bite into my right forearm. Blood dripped from my wound into my eyes. A scream of pain escaped my throat.

Thorlton plunged his claws into its neck. The wounded Wanderer jerked its head and scuttled off to the side. It growled at Thorlton, who bravely growled back.

Hollinshead shot an arrow, narrowly missing an advancing Wanderer. The arrow, though, distracted it long enough that she could help me up.

I grabbed Thorlton's arm and we followed Hollinshead into the bedroom, slamming the door behind us, our shoulders pressed against the wood. There was so much commotion on the other side, it sounded like a raging battle. We heard shrieks and yelps, flesh ripping and bones breaking.

Thump! Something was thrown hard against a wall. Every sound that came through the door made me consider my own death.

And then it was quiet. I slowly pressed my ear to the door, confused and distrusting the silence. I jumped when something struck the other side with a loud bang. We slowly stepped backwards, our eyes locked on the doorknob, willing it not to turn. We would have kept walking forever if it weren't for the far wall of the windowless room. We stood next to each other, holding our breath.

Hollinshead shielded me with her arm as the doorknob, squeaking loudly, slowly turned. After what felt like an eternity, the door opened.

STOLAS

My head was a bit woozy and a thrum was developing between my ears.

Our shoes left prints in the smeared blood as we cautiously exited the bedroom. We stepped between mangled corpses, many with broken necks.

A tall demon in a black robe stood at the other side of the room, his sunken eyes searching. His grey skin was broken by red fissures and he had two long horns.

I held my bleeding arm up to my chest. Hollinshead, showing a rare motherly concern, helped me remove my button-up shirt and tie it around my wound to apply pressure. I was now just wearing a bloody T-shirt that was glued to my body by sweat.

"It's not that deep," she said.

We looked over to Stolas, who was studying the bloated corpse at his feet.

"I can't believe it worked," Hollinshead said.

"Stolas. Sam. It's Stolas," Thorlton said.

I stepped forward, but I had no idea what to say to him. He didn't even seem to notice that we were in the room, or maybe he didn't care.

Say something. Harper needs him.

After a long pause, this is what came out of my mouth: "Soooooo, how ya doing?"

No reply. Instead, he stormed over to the door of the cabin and stopped, gazing at the world as if for the first time. He breathed in the air, and as he exhaled, his face twisted into a look of disgust.

"Let's move this along," Hollinshead said. She knocked me with her elbow, urging me to do something. I just shrugged, uncertain. Taking charge of the situation, she walked halfway to Stolas.

"Listen, buddy, Sam needs your help."

We heard growling and turned to look at Thorlton, who was in a tug of war with the cheek of a dead Wanderer. When our eyes returned to the door, Stolas was gone.

"He's chatty," I said, then turned to Hollinshead. "I guess our deal is done. You know about the red fog?"

She gave a slight nod, almost sorrowful.

"There's an inscription on the bottom of the box. It'll bring the fog," I said. "Just make sure you leave the box for me."

She smiled the biggest smile I'd ever seen, then ran to open her satchel. A few seconds later she said, "Something's wrong." Wood fragments filled her cupped hands.

"You've gotta be kidding me," I said. The box was destroyed. "It must have broken when I hit that thing in the head with your satchel."

Hollinshead balled her hand into a fist. I wasn't sure if I should apologize or run or cry.

"You idiot," she shouted.

"I'm sorry," I said. "I wasn't thinking."

She whipped the wood fragments at the wall. "When someone has a magic box, they should be a little more careful."

Hollinshead was right. In one moment, I had literally broken our only way of getting home. It's not like I hadn't broken a lot of stuff in my life — toys, my brother's Xbox, four or maybe even five bikes, an oven, two Blu-ray players, and, somehow, a garage door. Oh, and at least three of my phones had met a watery end in the bottom of a toilet bowl. The box wasn't some replaceable item, though. I had imagined Harper and me handing it to my uncle upon our safe return. He would happily add it to his private collection, removing the taint of my carelessness, give Harper a big hug, and forgive me for going against his wishes. That night, I'd tell him and Raymond all about my first real adventure.

Reality suffocated my fantasy. Hollinshead slowly walked toward me, her face clenched in anger. But her eyes revealed something else. Heartbreak.

"I'm a little stressed out," I yelled. "Harper's gone, I'm in Hell, Stolas is a bit standoffish, and now I can't get home either. The only one who seems to actually care is over in the corner, licking the corpse of a thing that tried to kill me."

"Thorlton!" Thorlton said, his arms high in celebration.

"No, Thorlton, I was just making a point."

Hollinshead threw me into a headlock and wrestled me to the ground. She straddled me, her strong hands squeezing my throat. Thorlton jumped back and forth, not sure which of us to help.

"I should have left you in Beleth," she said. Her hands tightened and my vision blurred.

"Enough," a voice said.

She loosened her grip. We both looked at Stolas standing by the door.

"More will come," he said.

We didn't speak much on our way to the sandy bank of a strong river. The grass under our feet was dry and trampled. All around us was calm, but I kept peering through the trees and bushes to see if something was lurking. I was more paranoid now than ever.

The results of my encounters with Banshees and Wanderers were showing on my left arm, chest, right hip, and cheek. Bruises were coming to the surface, on the cusp of colouring. I stood with Hollinshead, who looked defeated, and Thorlton, who muttered nervously. Stolas, his face and horns half-covered by the hood of his robe, paid no attention to us.

I had no idea how to start the conversation. It reminded me of the only date I had ever been on, which was so awkward that my mom apologized for me as she drove my date home.

We stood next to a wooden sign that read "Styx." A bullhorn blared, scaring a throng of creatures that dropped from the trees. Down the river, the bow of a black ship broke through the current, creating waves on each side. When it stopped in front of us, a demon boy with curly hair poking out of a blue sailor's hat dropped a wide plank for boarding.

Three-quarters of the ship was filled with benches where identical rowers sat. They looked half melted, like plastic soldiers that had been left under a magnifying glass on a sunny day. With every push and pull of the oars, agonized grunts rolled out of their sloped mouths.

We stood at the stern. My arm had stopped bleeding so I unwrapped it from my shirt. Scattered along the deck were a small handful of passengers. There was an older-looking demon with a liver-spotted face wrapped in a sheer headscarf. She sat on a wood block, fiddling with two knitting needles, creating something with stripes of pink and blue yarn. Next to her a muscular orange demon with scratch marks all over his body read a book. A lithe demon with beautiful black hair cascading down to her shoulders watched the river intently.

Hell's public transportation.

"Where are we going?" I asked.

"I'm getting off at the next stop," Hollinshead said.

"And what about you, Stolas? Where are you going?"

He looked at me out of the side of his dark eyes. Maybe that was a small victory.

"I'll stay, Sam. I'll stay. Find Harper," Thorlton said as he grabbed my hand.

"Harper?" Stolas said, his voice a deep baritone that lacked warmth. I had to replay it a few times in my head to make sure I didn't imagine it.

"She's the reason we rescued you," I said. "I need your help to find her."

Stolas's eyes focused on the oars that smacked the water.

I continued. "We went through a lot to find you. There were the mines, and before that we almost got killed by Pazuzu."

The last part caught his attention. I was hoping he would feel some sympathy and gratitude. Instead, he just studied me. I'd have been the first to admit this wasn't going well. It's not like I was expecting him to give me a high five and then we'd run off to save Harper, but it was moving too slowly for my liking. He was hard to decipher.

"Irekeep is my home. We'll go there," he said.

"Awesome. We can make a plan there." I was as excited as a small child.

The ship sailed under a drawbridge, its two halves slanting upwards. The same type of demon that operated the pulley system of the City of Belphegor oversaw the raising and lowering of the drawbridge.

We drifted past a quaint commune. Young demons sat on their knees at the edge of the river, dipping clothes into the water and scrubbing them on the ridged surfaces of washboards, a sweet sincerity on their faces. Older demons smoked pipes around a fire, the houses behind them connected by taut clotheslines. Some children weaved around trees. Two were duelling with branches, reminding me of my uncle, who, if he could see me, would be proud that I was riding along the Styx with my childhood hero.

"I was raised near this river," Stolas said. "Back-breaking work all day, harvesting wild grains. My only rest would be to get whipped. Years later, I sailed along this same river as a leader of demons. Not many slaves get that chance." He looked out over the calm water. "Look at it now. Filth everywhere."

I had no idea what he was talking about. The river looked fine to me.

Hollinshead was watching him with an expressionless, unwavering stare. I could tell she was feeling suspicious — I just didn't know of what.

"So what were you in the mines for?" Hollinshead asked. I started to answer, but she stopped me with a subtle raise of her hand, apparently curious to hear his answer instead.

"Not everyone appreciated my efforts to make this world great."

"Lack of appreciation seems like an odd reason to be sentenced to the worst prison in Hell," Hollinshead said.

"The mines weren't my gallows. I was there because of cowards with power."

"He's a hero," I said to her, the fanboy in me enthusiastically operating my mouth. Stolas then looked at me, sizing me up.

"My home is just outside Anais. Assuming it hasn't been ravaged by Volacs, we should arrive in a few hours."

Something seemed to be rattling around Hollinshead's brain.

The ship pulled into a port. The plank was dropped and the other passengers crossed it to shore. Several new ones boarded. I waited for Hollinshead to get off, but she just sat there, not showing even a hint of interest in leaving. I didn't know what had made her change her mind, but I was happy she was sticking around.

Hours passed before we disembarked in Anais, a place where everything was scarce except rotting wood. It was a quick walk from the port to the small city, so in no time we were strolling through streets of broken pavement, surrounded by houses and shops that needed a fresh coat of paint.

Thick-bodied Volacs went about their daily lives. They were known for two things: skin shedding and serpent riding. Stolas didn't seem to appreciate either quality, and I didn't want to run into a serpent big enough for these guys to ride.

The Volacs were shaped like Vikings, their red skin ravaged by what looked like shingles. The females wore dresses, shawls, and tight head wraps. The males wore tunics and loose trousers. I got a long look at a few of them who were crowded around a barrel, drinking water from a ladle. Close by, a merchant was selling purses and wallets that attracted only small insects to his booth. He spat into a puddle of saliva by his foot.

The smell of leather made me think of my first high-school dance. My mom had convinced me that I needed a night away from Cloaked Atlas, and my dad seconded her order. I spent the first hour of the dance listening to bad pop music and guarding a dozen leather purses along the wall of the gym. Finally, through a sea of bodies pulsing under a strobe light, I saw Harper. She pushed Kyle off her as she walked toward me. She took my hand and pulled me into the middle of the dance floor. We danced until Javier turned on the lights. We were the last two students in the gym. I didn't even care that I had to buy seven new purses.

We stopped to ask a Volac for a ride on his wagon but were met with a vulgar rejection. Stolas requested a word in private, and they went inside the Volac's house. Minutes later, only Stolas returned, telling us that the gentleman had offered his wagon as a kindness to strangers on a long journey.

Hollinshead, Thorlton, and I rode in the back of the wagon as Stolas manned the reins up front, the horse trotting briskly through a parched field. A gothic castle stood tall in the distance. That was Irekeep, the last home Stolas had known before he was robbed of his life. It was also the name of the blanket fort I'd built on more than one occasion.

"I don't trust him," Hollinshead said over the sound of the wheels rolling over rocks.

"You don't trust anyone. This guy freed like a million slaves and united the worst place ever, and that's still not enough for you."

"Right, 'cause that's what the good book told you," she said. "Take it from someone who's been wrong about a guy before, there's something up with him."

"Enough, Hollinshead," I said harshly. "If you want to leave, then leave."

The wagon clattered over some train tracks, the impact lifting us all from our seats. Sensing the tension, Thorlton shuffled over to sit between Hollinshead and me.

"I go with Sam. Harper."

Hollinshead gazed at the castle. We were quiet the rest of the way.

13
IREKEEP

The horse pulled to a stop in front of the castle. Slabs of creamy green mortar held grey stone together. Black flags rippled in the breeze. There were two spires but no moat or drawbridge. Even the surrounding forest was mostly stumps that didn't provide much protection. I guess if you were as beloved as Stolas, you weren't too concerned with intruders.

"Wait here," Stolas said. He hopped down from the wagon and disappeared inside the castle.

We stepped out of the wagon and awkwardly stood in front of the enormous wooden doors with metal knobs. Hollinshead was on highest alert. I didn't get why she was acting this way.

After a long while, the doors creaked open. We entered the impressive foyer with a luxurious carpet and varnished dark wood. A candelabra hung above, its arms reaching toward the walls. Stairs ran up each side of the room and met under bay windows. Stolas stood before us, his stare even more piercing than before.

"Find a room and I will see you in the morning," he said, then turned to leave.

"What about Harper?" I asked, but he must not have heard me as he headed down a flight of stairs at the end of a corridor.

"We're gonna connect later," I said to Hollinshead.

She shook her head at me.

At the end of the upstairs hallway we found two unlocked rooms, each with one bed. Hollinshead scurried into one room and slammed the door shut. Thorlton and I took the other.

Once inside, I slipped under the covers and Thorlton curled up at the end of the bed like a dog. In less than a minute, he was snoring like a chain smoker with sleep apnea. Not long after, I drifted off to sleep. We hadn't slept since Ragewick and I couldn't fight the exhaustion any longer.

I awoke in the dead of the night. I must have been in the middle of a bad dream, but then again, a dark room in an old castle felt like the setting for a bad dream. The wound on my arm reminded me that the last few days had really happened. Everything was real.

I checked on Thorlton, who was still soundly asleep, then I left the room. In my grogginess, my legs felt heavy and the hallway swayed as I returned to the darkened main floor. It was the kind of dark that tricked your brain into thinking there was something lurking behind the walls.

I stood at the top of the stairs where Stolas had left us. They spiralled down many more floors, making me wonder how deep into the ground this castle went and why that was even necessary. I started walking down.

I stopped on a lower floor, in a corridor lit by flames, with arched doors on both sides. Between the rooms hung framed oil paintings, each one depicting a scene of torture — heads being sawed off, limbs torn, tongues cut out. There was always a figure in the background, watching. I wasn't much of an art guy, but these paintings were weird. I never knew a still image could make me feel that uneasy.

One door was slightly ajar. Through the sliver of the opening I could see a room illuminated by fire. Shadows danced on the wall, creating a moving black portrait of three figures on their stomachs with their hands and feet hog-tied. I reached to open the door wider, but I was stopped by an even voice saying my name. It had come from a room at the other end of the corridor. I cautiously walked toward the flickering flame of a red candle.

This room was colder and more spacious than the other rooms. The three windows were simply big square holes carved into the wall, revealing an interrupted view of the outside.

"Don't mind him, he's the personal cipher for Irekeep," Stolas said, referring to the winged creature chained to the ground. He looked beaten, one of his wings cut off at the tip.

Stolas, his face half-covered by a brandy snifter, looked like royalty. He was wearing a black jacket and sitting in a wingback chair at the far end of a long table covered by a deep-purple tablecloth. He placed the snifter on the table and returned to his plate, on which raw meat sat in a pool of light-coloured blood. There was something odd about the way he delicately cut the meat as blood oozed out.

"Sit," he said. "Tell me, what do you know about the girl you travel with?"

"Not much." Why was he curious about Hollinshead? I slumped in the chair next to him.

He got up and filled a chalice to the brim and placed it in front of me. I drank it. The briny liquid burned my throat.

"Tell me, why did you really come to Hell?"

"To save my friend."

He smiled, not a pleasant smile, not the comforting kind, not even the kind that Hollinshead would throw my way, a smile of pity. There was something hidden beneath it. Bitterness.

"Those who are brought to Hell are mourned, not rescued, Sam." He walked around the room, making a show of circling me. "You must be running from something."

I had nothing to say. He probably wasn't interested in hearing about my dad or how an entire school was bullying me. I had to change the subject.

"Who's in the room down the hall?" I said.

"Oh, them. I don't know their names but they should never have been here. Irekeep is my home."

He stared out of the window, onto his land.

"I've been forgotten," Stolas said.

He walked back to the table and ran his finger along his plate, catching a dollop of the watery blood. He placed it on his lips. His mouth formed a smile that looked like a knife slice from cheek to cheek.

"All my blood to make this world pure. It was all for nothing."

"I thought peace was your thing?" I said.

"I'm pleased that my legacy wasn't lost on you," he said. "Why do you want my help?"

"'Cause in those stories you were fearless and selfless, and I know I can't do this alone."

His eyes latched on to mine. He mulled over my response.

"You know I was a slave, but do you know what the heart of the slave truly desires?

"To be free."

"To be the one cracking the whip."

A vein pulsed between his horns. Red took hold of his slate grey eyes. In only a moment, his face had twisted into something sinister. I was taken aback. His behaviour and words contradicted the version of him that leaped from the pages of *The Book of Stolas*. The one that lived in my head. I gripped the arms of my chair with sweaty palms. My anxiety was spiralling out of control.

"This is a godless world, poisoned by all the lessers that came to my shores, those who sought to dilute us." He looked deep into my eyes. "You sit in a room in a castle built by slaves. I never saw the value in the freedom of others."

Oh crap. Hollinshead was right.

I wanted to leave but there was only one way out of the room, and at that moment it felt miles away.

"Ya know, I have a lot of wacky ideas," I said. "Why don't we put a pin in this? We'll get out of your hair and you can go back to whatever it is you do." I stood up, but before I could take a step, he placed a hand on my shoulder and forced me back into the chair.

A familiar and awful smell slithered under the stone wall. I heard long nails scrapping. My eyes followed the sound until it stopped. The rock crumbled, the wall split open, and on the other side stood Pazuzu. He smiled when our eyes met. My brain jumped back to Beleth and the image of him as that creature crawling along the roof. My chest felt close to exploding. I was trapped.

"Why would you do this?" I asked Stolas, hurt.

"I made a deal, and you and the girl were the price I had to pay."

We turned to the sound of struggle coming from the corridor. Out of the dark and into the orange glow of the room, Hollinshead was thrown onto the floor, landing on her stomach. Cerberus appeared out of the darkness, sporting a dramatic scowl.

As Hollinshead crawled toward me, Cerberus kicked her hard, flipping her onto her back. She gurgled some blood and spat it out. I hated seeing her in pain.

Pazuzu crouched next to Hollinshead and ran his fingers through her knotted, sweaty hair.

"We had a fair arrangement," he said. The hairs on the back of my neck stood to attention as I listened. "How many slaves would have to suffer for you to get what you want?"

I was floored. Hollinshead, my saviour, had been helping that monster.

"I like to imagine the moment. A slave stops to enjoy some well-earned freedom, believing they are safe, only to be snatched back by our friend here," Pazuzu said with an awful smile. His words drew a smile from Stolas as well.

My uncle's voice crawled into my ear. *There's no one in any world who is perfectly good.*

Hollinshead looked full of regret, the look anyone has when their darkest secret is revealed.

"Is this true?" I asked. She looked at me, her eyes vacant for the first time since I had met her.

Pazuzu pushed me against the wall. Cerberus grabbed Hollinshead's shirt and slammed his fist into her face, his two smaller heads cackling with glee. A trail of blood leaked out of her nose and her cheek split open.

"Bring them back to Beleth," Pazuzu said.

"Sam. Sam. Hollinshead." Thorlton's raspy voice broke through the dark of the corridor.

He stood right in the middle of everyone. He cocked his head, trying to piece the scene together. Maybe it was the blood on Hollinshead's face or the hand on my throat, but something turned his doe eyes fierce. He clenched his little fists and growled so loudly that the silverware on the table shook. Like a rabid animal, Thorlton hurled himself at Pazuzu's head. He scratched viciously at his face and bit into his neck. Blood seeped down Pazuzu's back.

Hollinshead was coming to. She held her sore ribs and spat out a gob of blood.

Pazuzu screamed as he stumbled around trying to shake Thorlton loose. He fell back onto the table, knocking the candles and alcohol over, giving birth to a fire that danced on the puddles.

Seizing the opportunity, Hollinshead pulled herself off the floor, picked up a candle, and ran toward Stolas.

She jumped on top of him, throwing him to the ground. He tried to knock the candle out of her hand, but she thrust the flame into his face, searing his eye. I expected him to scream, but he only became enraged.

Flames travelled up Stolas's jacket. Cerberus grabbed Hollinshead's arms from behind. She slammed her head back, bending his nose. He yowled in pain and let go of her, then stumbled backwards toward the window. With full force, Hollinshead ran at him and drove her shoulder into his chest, throwing him out the window.

I grabbed Thorlton's arm and ran behind Hollinshead out of the room, which was now filled with rising fire and a cloud of thick smoke. We made it to the end of the hallway and instinctively flew down the spiral steps that descended into the bowels of the castle. The path to the bottom felt like it would never end.

Finally, we arrived at the lowest level, a dank dungeon completely hidden from the world above. It smelled like a subway station bathroom. As we walked past the cells, we saw the rotting remains of different demons, many crawling with fat maggots.

"How do we get out of here?" Hollinshead said, her face betraying her fear. She stared at the skeletal remains of a prisoner that had been left to rot.

"Maybe we should head back up and try to find another way out," I said.

"Tsk, tsk," a soft voice said from the other end of the dungeon.

A melodic whistling enticed us to come closer. We followed it until we discovered a demon sitting at a small desk in a cell, quill in hand and a stack of papers in front of him.

"Stolas was a crafty one. Knew what he was doing when he had Irekeep built. So many passageways and secret doors, means of escape if his enemies were to ever find him. He was a demon with many enemies. Did you know that Gary and Dashiell captured him in this very castle?" The prisoner stood up and approached the bars. He slid his arms through them as he leaned forward, pointing at me. "He was standing right where you are, screaming that they were going to sentence him. He tried to escape, even asked for our help. That was a laugh, the executioner asking the damned for help."

"What do you mean 'our'?" I asked.

"My brethren. My fellow prisoners."

"Um … pretty sure everyone else is dead," I said.

"Huh. That would explain why no one responded to my escape plans."

Hollinshead grabbed the bars of his cell. "Got a way out of here?" she said eagerly.

"Release me and I'll show you a way out."

Hollinshead and I looked at each other. Her mistrust was infectious. I couldn't quiet that voice in my head that warned me against releasing another demon from a prison. He might be a prisoner, but he was holding all the power.

The ceiling shook above us. For a second, I had a flashback to Belphegor and the feeling of being in a moving city.

"Did I mention my way out leads directly to train tracks?" The prisoner smiled knowingly.

Hollinshead's decisiveness took charge. She took the gold pin out of her pocket, the one we were given in

Ragewick, and fiddled the sharp tip into the lock until it opened. The prisoner threw on his ratty jacket and placed his papers and a quill into a cracked messenger bag, which he then slung over his shoulder.

He stepped out of the cell and stretched his arms. His outfit looked old and decidedly British: a dark-blue jacket and pants, a matching vest, and buckled shoes. He placed a hat between his grey horns, covering his wavy black hair.

Thorlton hopped onto my shoulder, and we followed the prisoner to the far wall of the dungeon. He stood in front the large interlocking stones.

"I watched that bastard do this a thousand times," he said as he pressed a sequence of stones like keys on a piano. Each stone turned a light shade of red as he pushed it into the wall. After he had touched the last stone, he stepped back and we waited.

"Quick question, who are we running from?" the prisoner asked.

"Let's talk later," Hollinshead said.

Racing footsteps echoed into the dungeon. The three of us stared at the prisoner, who bounced pleasantly on his heels. The footsteps grew louder. Voices travelled down, speaking of what horrors they would do once they caught us. The word *maim* carried the loudest.

"Stolas?" the prisoner asked. "It can't be."

We looked back at the wall. The stones were pulling apart, creating an opening, along with the feeling that maybe I could get out of this alive even though I had no idea what was waiting on the other side.

A gust of wind blew into the dungeon from the opening, carrying faint groans and the pungent stench of embalmment. There was no time to process anything. The footsteps were getting closer. The prisoner calmly stepped to the side and lowered himself to a bow.

"Ladies first," he said.

Hollinshead led the way into the dark, with the prisoner acting as caboose. Not far behind, we could hear our pursuers running across the dungeon. Burning red eyes shone from the dirt walls, lighting our path. Cold fingers touched our bodies. I could hear whispered conversations. I tried to only look forward, to stay focused on the hope of an exit, dreading the thought that a strange hand could grab me at any moment.

The prisoner had told us that Stolas had many enemies. Someone with a lot of enemies needed many dungeons, and it was clear that we were running through one of his more inventive ones.

More red eyes popped open. I recoiled but had to keep running toward the sound of a chugging train.

Light broke through a mess of branches and muddy leaves that covered the exit. Without hesitation, Hollinshead burst through, clearing the way.

The train rumbled behind us, closing the gap with every second. Its wide chimney released a constant, thick trail of black steam. The wheels, cylinders, and connecting rods all engaged in a fluid movement that disturbed the ground and rattled the tracks.

We ran through straw, around stumps and over decomposing animals. Our pace quickened to a sprint as the first train car thundered past us.

Each car had long horizontal windows and an opening with a metal railing, meant to allow passengers quick access to board. Of course, they were designed with the assumption that the train would be idling in a station. How I was going to catch the railing as Hollinshead had just done?

Hollinshead stepped onto the landing and secured herself in the opening. She extended her arms, catching Thorlton, who had jumped from my shoulder. The prisoner ran by me and managed to leap onto the train.

I didn't have much energy left; my body had already been through a lot. Hollinshead leaned farther out, her shirt flapping wildly in the gale. I couldn't hear what she was saying over the noise, but her face was red from the force of yelling.

Scenes from back home flashed through my mind. I was sitting on my bed, Harper next to me. She held her phone to my face. My brain made the words bigger, bolder, and even more ominous than they were the first time I saw them: *Fag, Loser, Lame.* The wounds of these words deepened every time I thought about them, but this time they made my legs move faster. My uncle's voice filled my head, telling me to focus on the jump. Even though missing would mean I could be pulled under the train, I jumped to the side, barely catching the railing. The wind lifted me, forcing me against the side of the train, which was picking up speed at the worst time. Only a shaky railing kept me from joining the dead animals that blurred below.

My sweaty hand stung from my tight hold on the metal. Against my will, my grasp started to ease. My heart stopped as I slipped off. But before I could shoot away, Hollinshead caught my wrist. Even she was struggling to keep me from certain death.

My wrist slid out of her hand, leaving only our fingers connected. She planted her feet and leaned back, trying to pull me toward her. There was no quit in her, but her effort was pointless. Our fingers began to separate.

The window above me slid open and out poked the head of the prisoner. His long arms wrapped around my body like tentacles. He pulled me through the window, and we both fell to the floor of the train.

The prisoner and I sat there, trying to catch our breath. I was also trying not to think about everything that had just happened. He leaned against the wall, drumming on his knees, stopping only once to wink at me. He stood up and held out his hand.

"Shall we?" he asked. I took his hand and lifted myself to my feet.

Through a doorway, we found Hollinshead and Thorlton. They stood in silence, looking at me with a pity I was all too familiar with. Even Thorlton was at a loss for words.

In that moment, when we should have all finally felt safe, all I could feel was dread. I had made a terrible mistake.

THE HOLLOWS LIMITED

The *Hollows Limited* was loud and rhythmic. I could feel every chug as we walked down the corridor. The prisoner found an empty sleeper cabin and we snuck in behind him. The plush benches squeaked as we flopped down.

Hollinshead and Thorlton were feeling the crash after their adrenalin rush. It took them only a few minutes to fall asleep next to each other. As Hollinshead drifted off, she snorted about how only I would bring the worst guy back to life.

I stared at Thorlton, who looked so peaceful, but I couldn't help but think of him attacking Pazuzu. It struck me how attached to us he had become. Showing Thorlton just a little bit of kindness had earned us his full loyalty.

The prisoner asked me to join him on a walk through the train. I followed him down a long carpet, sneaking quick glances into cabin windows. One caught my attention. A scrawny demon with soft eyes was stroking the hair of another demon who lay with his head on his lap. They looked happy, enjoying the ride through a blur of towns and a mountain range. They reminded me of my uncle and Raymond. This was the Hell that Stolas hated so much.

My uncle had been wrong about The Books of Hell, and so had I. These stories had been my unofficial guide through a strange world, but I couldn't trust them anymore. I had lost my only advantage.

"So Stolas is back," the prisoner said. "I did not see that coming."

"We rescued him from the mines. I thought he could help me."

He stopped and gave me a look that I was relieved wasn't accompanied by words. He let out a hearty laugh and continued walking. Frustration boiled inside of me.

I wish I'd never found that stupid book.

"A daring escape from the City of Belphegor? Sounds thrilling."

"Who are you?" I asked.

"The name's Moscow Woodwick Felipe Ransom."

He said his name the way most propose marriage, with flair and cheerful inflection.

"I'm Sam."

"Sam. Yes, I like that name. It's just odd enough to be memorable. And the girl and the little one?"

"Hollinshead and Thorlton."

"Delightful."

Moscow took off his hat and brushed the brim with his hand. He had confidence and swagger, as if his time in prison had been just a pit stop. The gentle lilt in his voice was appealing.

"Why were you a prisoner?"

"A long story, my friend, one that should be told over a drink — many, many drinks," he said. "This might be stating the obvious, but you don't look as if you're from these parts. Berdymian, correct?"

"Long story as well."

He walked backwards so he could take stock of me, then spun back around.

"I'm looking for someone. I thought Stolas could help me, but now I'm screwed," I said.

"Must be someone special."

"She is."

"Well, you were grossly misled about Stolas. Fret not, it happens to the best of us. Who convinced you of that ridiculous theory?"

"*The Book of Stolas.* Once I found out that Hell was real, I thought those stories were as well. I'm such an idiot." I dropped my head into my hands, embarrassed at hearing my explanation out loud. Moscow smiled.

"Sam, right now we drink and enjoy a taste of freedom. Plenty of time later for stories, laughter, tears, and all that," he said.

We entered the long dining car, which rocked with life and smelled like burning coal and stale beer. After a few minutes, the stench became bearable. Drunks stood at cruiser tables, laughing and chatting as they smacked their glasses on the tables, booze dripping onto the already stained carpet. What looked like four old friends were sitting in a booth, smoking hand-rolled cigarettes and sharing green liquid from a thin-necked bottle. A short demon with a garish smile danced on the bar, kicking the air.

To get the bartender's attention, Moscow tapped the wooden bar twice. The bartender, who wore a shirt that read "Can't Talk, Gotta Rum," had the neck of a giraffe, which he craned to fit his shrunken head under the ceiling. He looked at Moscow, who, with a showman's flourish, pointed to a bottle on the top shelf. The bartender removed the bottle, popped out the cork, poured the blue liquid into a glass, and slid it right into Moscow's anxious hand. While he nursed his drink, smiling with each sip, I scarfed down handfuls of the salty snacks that were in small bowls along the bar. I hadn't eaten since the cabin and was starting to feel the effects of hunger. I also couldn't help but wonder how we were going to pay the tab.

"It's the little things you miss," Moscow said, staring deep into the blue drink. "Legend has it that the Krauss cured themselves of grey boil fever with this very brew. I simply enjoy the buzz."

After he finished his drink at the bar, we sat in a banquette, a straight line of shot glasses between us. In his left hand, Moscow clutched a quarter-full bottle. In his right was an unlit cigar, the end tattered as if it had been lit and put out many times.

Framed by the windows, the countryside flew by. The swoosh of colour and the flurry of towns and rivers was like watching the world through a kaleidoscope lens. One image stung the back of my eyes. On a long golden plain, a cloaked Hanbi calmly stood in front of a red hole, out of which wisps of fog swirled. A young boy, strangled by red fog, was brought through the hole and deposited at the Hanbi's feet. I watched as the sobbing boy was dragged toward the horizon.

"We're all still playing in their world," Moscow said. He threw back a shot, then poured one for me.

"Who?"

"Alchem, Emperor Belphegor, and, let's not forget, Stolas. It's always the bad ones who shape us."

Moscow leaned back, his arm stretched across the top of the booth. The bottom of his shirt was starting to untuck.

"Take Alchem, for instance, awful demon, that one. So eager to preserve the Hanbi way of life that he offered the emperor gifts made of his own blood, gifts that connected our worlds — and not for the better," Moscow said. "One selfish act led to the Rhinedack slave trade, expedited the crowning of an emperor, and is why your *special someone* was taken from her home. The ripple of life can be abhorrent, if you ask me."

"And what about Stolas?" I said.

"What about him?" He tipped the front of his top hat up. He stared at me, not in an intimidating way, but offering me the opportunity to withdraw my request.

"Everything made him sound like a legend."

"You mean the Battle of the Great Falling City and those heartfelt speeches on the Riverway?" He waved his hand as if to shoo away his thoughts. It angered me. "A great storyteller can sell any story, Sam. They're just words, but someone who feels wronged will find purpose in mere words."

Moscow looked both bothered and drunk.

"How do you know this?" I asked.

Moscow placed the palm of his hand on the shot glass that was rocking back and forth from the motion of the train. He whistled and held two fingers up to the bartender, signalling to bring us a couple more drinks.

"How do you know they're lies?" I asked again, this time more forcefully.

Moscow paused dramatically.

"Because I wrote them," he said.

A memory blossomed. That night in Cloaked Atlas when I found that dusty copy of *The Book of Stolas*, the initials *M.W.F.R.* written in beautiful cursive. Moscow Woodwick Felipe Ransom.

I tried to weave together the threads of what I thought I knew and what I had just learned, but my head was a jumbled mess. I was staring at the demon who, without knowing it, had changed my life. The one who had manipulated me into coming to Hell and convinced me to find Stolas.

"I didn't have a choice," Moscow said. He took a deep breath as if to give himself time to organize the beats of his story in his head. "I was a lowly writer spinning beautiful words into tales of romance that I sold from town to town. One night, I sat alone at an inn, enjoying some Perry cider, when an Arkavelle shoved a hood over my head. I was thrown onto a cart and listened to the sound of a horse trotting for hours until I found myself at Irekeep. I was told that the only thing that would keep my head attached to my body was to be Stolas's narrator. Not long after the ink had dried on the last word in *The Book of Stolas*, I had codified a monster."

He leaned forward, his mouth close to my ear. "This might be weird to ask, I realize, but did you like the book?"

I dropped my forehead onto the table, feeling like a complete screw-up. I didn't want him to see that I was holding back tears, which were making my vision misty.

I'd thought Stolas was a hero, I really did. I imagined his actions and victories as if they were godly, the kind of deeds that would get passed down from generation to generation as the gold standard of bravery.

The bartender brought over two shots, and Moscow sent him back with an order for another two.

"You want to know the real Stolas?" he asked. "He understood the wheels that turned Hell. He knew that deposing an emperor would win him fame, but what he truly craved was legacy. To achieve that, he had to be a god to the commoners, the ones who tell stories around the fire to their little ones, the ones who, if they ever found their collective voice, could overthrow an empire. That was the difference. Emperor Belphegor might have built a city, but Stolas built a world."

My mistake was even more severe than I'd thought. I hoped I wasn't the only sucker in Hell. Moscow lit his cigar and then continued.

"He held a candle up to the darkness of demons — their hate, their fear. He knew exactly how to manipulate the ones who had suffered so much. He could sell a horse to a Dampier."

I shrugged, confused by his reference.

"Dampiers. The horseless ones. Anyway, Stolas did help in removing the emperor, but he was driven by selfishness, a desire to be Hell's iron fist. Within that void of power, Stolas made alliances. All his opponents, including the Architects, were either exiled or murdered. He used fear as a weapon to persecute any demon or race that he deemed unfit. He doubled the Rhinedack slave trade. He stomped on the throats of the oppressed."

I took a shot glass and threw the liquid into the back of my mouth. He smiled at me, which made me feel a bit better.

"As he grew his own legend, immense crowds would fill the Riverway just to hear him speak," he said.

His eyes focused out the window. Gobsmacked by my own stupidity, I reached to take another shot, but Moscow gently grabbed my wrist. "It's a long trip, my boy."

I put down the glass. I started thinking about what Pazuzu had told me about Hollinshead. Justified or not, I felt betrayed. How could she return innocent people to that monster? What if it had been Harper who had run? I knew the answer and it hurt.

"My uncle once told me there was no one perfectly good in any world," I said.

"A wise man, I'm sure, but I like to think that there's no world perfectly bad." Moscow blew out a smoke ring. I couldn't believe those words were coming out of the mouth of someone who not long ago was living in a dirt cell surrounded by skeletons. "Hell is war and famine, villages where children are hung by their feet because their mother stole to feed them," he said. "There are cities built on the beaten backs of slaves. River beds so full of corpses that they are graveyards."

Moscow paused for a second, and a subtle smile flashed across his face. "But that's not the Hell I know. It is a place of love and friendship and song. It is demons from other worlds coming together to rebuild their lives. It was a new world that provided hope, and that hope will always be its bedrock."

He left the table, returning a few minutes later with a couple more bowls of snacks. He urged me to keep eating until we had time and money for a proper meal. Based on the journey so far, who knew when that would be? We each placed some food in a napkin and put them in our pockets to bring back for Hollinshead and Thorlton.

"You came to Hell looking for someone special, right?" Moscow asked.

"Her name's Harper."

"And Harper is a friend or something more?"

I paused, searching for an answer. Moscow seemed to pick up on my apprehension.

"The reason I ask is that the other one keeps sneaking looks at you. Looks I used to be very familiar with."

I was caught off guard by his remark, especially since Hollinshead's eyes usually darted away from mine when I looked at her.

He raised an eyebrow and smiled. "Plus, there was the whole almost-falling-out-of-a-moving-train-to-save-you business."

I was super thankful when this conversation was interrupted by a large woman flopping down next to me, her face splotchy from gobs of makeup and her head weighed down by an intricate hairdo. She flashed a red-wine-coloured smile as her eyes shifted between Moscow and me.

"Who's this looker?" she asked, pointing at me.

Before I could answer, Moscow piped up. "This is Sam. I'm sure you have heard of him."

She gave me a sideways glance.

"Come now! You must have heard of the great Sam, the Liberator of Belphegor." Moscow stepped onto the table as the crowd quieted.

He pointed at me. "This man here, the one with the dirty cheeks and tousled hair, the one who smells of sweat and puberty, it was he who whispered to the Banshee. It was he who stared the great falling city in its unforgiving eye and scoffed at its dangers." He grabbed my arm and pulled me up on the table next to him.

"Sam, tell us your tale," Moscow said. "Tell us how you performed such heroic feats." He softly stepped down from the table and wedged himself between two demons, who, along with everyone else, were staring at me. I could feel the temperature in the room rise and my shirt collar tighten like a noose.

A storyteller can sell any story.

I stood in front of the crowd, took a deep breath, and launched into my story. As I spoke, my nerves melted. I told the entire room about first arriving in Hell, about the escape from Beleth, about combing through the Mines of Belphegor in search of bones (never mentioning Stolas's name, mind you). I told them about the daring climb to safety and battling with the Wanderers. I ended with the escape from a madman's castle. The smiles of my listeners widened with every sentence. If I had been in the audience, I would have been smiling, too. I finished my story to rousing applause that made me feel as drunk as Moscow was in that moment. One audience member was so swept away by my words that he paid our bill.

Hours passed as *The Hollows Limited* rattled along tracks that curled around a mountain like a serpent would its prey, then propelled us into the darkness of tunnels. As the alcohol flowed, the room opened up with cursing, laughter, and raised glasses. Moscow and I sang and danced along with all the creatures and demons. The entire car wanted nothing more than a good time. It felt like a small treasure on a journey that had caused me so much pain.

Moscow taught me the songs of Panthos, his home-land, and I received so many pats on the back and handshakes that I felt as if I had won the big game or was celebrating my bar mitzvah. Whenever someone asked me about the person I was searching for in Belphegor, Moscow would sidle in and perfectly deflect the conversation back to my heroics. It worked every time.

After a while, most of the drunken passengers were either slumped at the bar or flat on the floor. The crowd thinned as some made their way to their sleeper cars. I put my arm around Moscow's waist and he put his arm around my shoulders, and we walked through the rocking train. His movements lacked coordination, yet he still spoke with perfect eloquence, as if his brain were impenetrable to alcohol.

"You can ignore this question, since I know it's a sore spot, but did you like the book? There were times when I felt I was capturing the story. Other times not so much," he said as we stumbled into our car, waking up Hollinshead in the process.

Hollinshead pulled herself up from her nap, her eyes barely open, hair mussed. She gave me a suspicious look as she stretched.

"Are you guys drunk?" she asked.

There wasn't much sense in denying it. My hands were a bit shaky, but my body felt light for the first time since arriving in Hell.

"It's a pleasure to formally make your acquaintance. The name is Moscow Woodwick Felipe Ransom." He grabbed Hollinshead's hand and kissed it.

The motion of the train jolted Thorlton awake. He gnawed at his ankle, mistaking it for an attacking enemy. After a minute, we were able to calm him down.

"So, my little friend, where are you from?" Moscow asked Thorlton.

"Mara. Mara."

"Dreadful town. No atmosphere. And you, Hollinshead? I mean besides Berdym."

"Around," she replied.

"Judging by the mark on your wrist, I'm guessing you've spent a bit of time in Beleth."

Hollinshead dipped her head toward him and gave him a half-hearted salute. Even Moscow's charm couldn't convince her to open up about her past.

"Where to from here?" he said.

"I need to find Harper and figure out a way home," I said, looking at Hollinshead, who returned a faint smile.

"Tell me how the girl was brought to Hell," Moscow said.

"I was tricked into opening one of Alchem's Gifts by a demon named Moloch."

"I see. Well, then, it's quite simple. Moloch was most likely working for someone, so if we find him, he will lead us to Garbo."

"Harper," I said, correcting him.

"Even better!"

"How do we find Moloch?" Hollinshead said, obviously intrigued by Moscow's plan.

"We visit a Leper Monk," he said.

"Gary," I said.

"Yes, and don't worry, Sam, I didn't write that one," he said, referring to *The Book of Gary*. Funny guy.

The Book of Gary described its subject as the most powerful of his kind and the first demon that Evelynn approached when she formed the Architects.

It felt good to have the beginning of a new plan, but I was worried that it would just give me another chance to mess things up.

That evening, we arrived in Kastrip Luccos, a dust bowl made up of four unpaved streets, one leading in each direction. The main road featured Mabel's Tavern, its slanted sign hanging over the door, bookended by a general store and a cipher's office. Just before the train came into the station, I saw a white brick schoolhouse where the teacher was holding class on the front lawn. The town looked as if the residents had lost a bet.

The train pulled to a stop as steam shrieked out of the smokestack and wafted through the open-air station. We exited along with hundreds of other passengers onto the wooden platform. I looked up at *The Hollows Limited*, a magnificent beast that maintained its dramatic allure even when motionless.

The railway staff removed luggage from the baggage car. Five porters walked through the station with large burlap sacks over their shoulders.

A crush of commuters roamed the platform, searching for their luggage or travel companions. I remembered my time in Mara and how I felt like a total outsider when I first stood among the citizens of this world. Everything felt a little less strange now.

"Where's Moscow?" Hollinshead said.

I pointed to the end of the train, where Moscow was rummaging through pieces of luggage that sat unattended. He opened a bag and took out some of the items. He stuffed a gold pocket watch, a light brown wallet, and an assortment of jewellery into his pockets.

He sauntered over to us, only stopping to doff his hat at a pretty creature twirling a yellow parasol. She was taken by his charm.

"The next leg of our journey will be on foot, so we should get moving," Moscow said.

We navigated through the crowd of hugging demons and others asking the staff for directions. Close by, a young demon, short and with tiny horns, tugged on her father's beard as he playfully egged her on.

We crossed the threshold into the lavish terminal, footsteps echoing throughout its vastness. Shiny black and white tiles were fitted together to create a pattern on the floor. White marble columns reached all the way to the ceiling, which was made entirely of stained glass. Between the columns were powder-coated steel benches. It reminded me of Union Station in Toronto and of walking through the grand terminal and across the glass SkyWalk to go watch a Blue Jays game. My parents would take me, and every time we walked out of the SkyWalk, my dad would point to the CN Tower and tell me about how he once saw Mick Jagger eating in its revolving restaurant.

The four of us left the terminal and started to trek over the plains. The only sound was the squawking of birds above us. It took effort to flatten the tall grass as we strode, making me wonder if we were the first to ever walk this part of Hell.

I thought of Kyle and of how, no matter where I went, I always carried that pain with me. One memory was crowned monarch in my mind. Years before the Snapchat incident, my gym class was playing kickball. I was at bat, and I wound up to wallop the ball all the way to what I thought would be the parking lot. Instead, the ball meekly rolled off my heel and right into the pitcher's arm. From left field — which was more like shortstop because the entire outfield had moved in close — Kyle got his team to chant, "What a loser." Their taunts chased me off the field. He had this way of inspiring others to see me through his eyes, of using their insecurities to get what he wanted. That night, after I had cried for an hour, my mom dropped me off at Cloaked Atlas, hoping it would cheer me up. I spent the night in the reading nook with my uncle, an open book on his lap. That was the first time I heard about Stolas, a slave who, despite being whipped and demeaned from the time he could walk, grew to rule a world with courage and kindness. He was a testament to a strength that went far beyond kicking a ball.

I walked with Moscow, cigar between his teeth. In front were Hollinshead and Thorlton. She had become even more distant since Irekeep, probably because she didn't want to talk about what she had done. I was glad to be behind her because now, thanks to Moscow, I was very aware that she might be looking at me at any given time.

I was disgusted with myself for having freed Stolas and for thinking that he was going to help me. Sensing my mood, Moscow placed a hand on my shoulder. We stopped walking and stood on the plains, staring off into the distance.

"He fooled thousands before you, Sam. You shouldn't feel any shame."

He reached into his messenger bag and thumbed through a stack of paper.

"Here," he said, handing me some pages, most of which were torn.

"What this?"

"Something I've been working on. Read it," Moscow said.

I read it. And every word ripped my heart out.

Excerpt from *The Truth About Stolas*
Written by M.W.F.R.

The empire had fallen, yet the promise of peace remained unfulfilled. The oppressed still felt unheard and even more marginalized. The shores filled with ships of foreigners looking for opportunity, but instead, they were met with only hate and servitude.

A group of writers were tasked as narrators. Their job was to inspire the masses through the stories of each Architect in a series entitled The Books of Hell. Despite his excessive lobbying, and due to his behaviour during the restoration, Stolas was denied the honour.

What does one obsessed with legacy do when faced with the prospect of being forgotten? One writes one's own book, of course.

Swarms would gather in the town squares and halls and all along the river to hear Stolas speak. They were packed so tight that not even a sliver of daylight could break through the bodies.

I could always be found in the front row, recording the events under the distasteful eye of Stolas's henchmen. Against my will, I was being forced to pen the depraved lie known as *The Book of Stolas*.

The moment when he took the wooden stage was always the same: a few scattered demons would shush the rest and then a deathly hush would fall upon the crowd. One could hear a pin drop as all eyes became fixed on the self-proclaimed Liberator of Belphegor.

Stolas would open with his humble beginnings as the only child of peasants, two unlucky Arkavelles who were forced to work hard labour in the Neeyson Valley. His voice would deepen, his eyes burn red as he spoke of his parents, who sold him into slavery.

He was always dressed in the garb of the townspeople: dirty and dented armour for the Krauss, a hooded surcoat of the finest silk for the crowd on The Spear, simple tunics for the Alpsecords — a message to his gatherers that he was one of them. He regaled the crowd with the efforts of the Architects, but his adulation painted a picture of a power-hungry, divided group. He taught all who listened that it was he alone who returned from Mount Anubis with Adramelech's Horn, it was he who used that horn to turn the Wanderers against their master, and it was his will that led the assault on the falling city. He had it perfectly rehearsed, right down to the dramatic pause just after he told them that it was his blade that had dripped with the emperor's blood, not the blade of Gary or that of Dashiell or that of Evelynn.

He spoke of the danger of idle words and how the dream of Hell was pure but had been poisoned by the reality of backdoor dealings, selfish alliances, and what many mistakenly called progress. He asked the crowd why they should be the victims of a caste system, stamped at birth to beg and suffer. His final promise was that they would never again have to kneel for a false emperor.

Stolas was masterful. The rapture was total.

His outpouring of vitriol touched every member of the crowd, and he was always met with applause, tears, and a legion of new followers. His followers would be so overcome with emotion and charged with righteousness that his words echoed long after in every home, alley, and tavern. All Stolas had to do was validate their frustration from afar.

Without payment, *The Book of Stolas* was written and became the song of the forgotten, a reminder for the unheard to raise a voice and a weapon against any demons who fancied themselves the next emperor.

Behind the rhetoric and hidden from public view was the deeply troubled mind of a slave who never forgot his first taste of power.

He left a trail of the dead on his march to Panthos. There, he burned the town to the ground and massacred the Krauss (although this fire, recorded as the great Panthos fire, was blamed on the careless slaves at the tannery).

His campaign continued to the Riverway, where his dissenters were drowned in the Gwyn River (recorded as the voluntary mass offering to Alchem). He was then off to the Neeyson

Valley, where he single-handedly murdered Abyzou's beloved daughters (recorded as the Neeyson slave uprising). They were buried in the valley.

The sirens of war were silent, but the horror and bloodshed were louder than anything Hell had ever experienced.

The Architects had to quell Stolas and his rising insurgency, but killing him would have only created a martyr. As they worked toward a plan, Stolas took an even more severe turn.

Evelynn's corpse was found in the bottom of a well in Mara.

Camio was beheaded in his sleep.

Ardat's family moved him to a secret location.

Gutsmith was burned at the stake before the demons of Tower Hill.

Gorgora was fed to the river monster known as the Kappa.

Gary went into self-exile.

Dorian was granted permission to live in the hidden land of the Alpsecords called the Nothingness.

Dashiell survived numerous attempts on his life before retreating to his lighthouse in Ep Sumter.

The Architects were no more. The only one who stood was the more powerful Stolas. It was a marvel to behold how one demon could plunge a bloodied world into even more turmoil.

Gary travelled in secret to meet with Dashiell. They agreed that Stolas had become more dangerous than Belphegor and that it would only be a matter of time before his influence grew. Gary's two conditions were that the killing had to cease and the laws needed to be upheld. This meant that Stolas would be spared death and justly sentenced based on his crimes.

Knowing that they could not outdo Stolas's talent for politics and rewriting history, they decided that it would take another battle to remove Hell from his grasp. Gary and Dashiell, along with an army made up of Volacs and Incubi and Succubi, surrounded Irekeep. The event officially commenced with a cluster of arrows raining upon the castle.

Stolas attempted an escape through his underground tunnel but was captured and taken to the City of Belphegor. Ciphers informed the world of his crimes.

In the streets of Belphegor, crowds shouted cheers that lasted for days as they basked in the announcement that their true oppressor had been brought to justice.

The pull of tightly wrapped chains removed Stolas's limbs. Guillotines cut off his feet, hands, and head. His skin was melted off and scattered across the rock. His bones were buried throughout the mine. Every one of his screams eased the suffering of the crowd.

No new copies of *The Book of Stolas* were ever to be printed. The first editions became rare collector's items, and a few were smuggled to Berdym and sold to collectors for astronomical prices.

Stolas's true life and nature was never recorded. Every effort was made to push the memory of him from public consciousness.

His name was spoken less and less with each passing year, and eventually he became nothing but a forgotten footnote in a dark period of history. So it happens that time makes one forget and the world changes, leaving behind only a faint trail of tales and forgotten lessons.

I handed the papers back to Moscow, shaken from learning the real history and how easily it had been twisted. I had believed in a monster and risked my life to save him. Worst of all, I had let Harper down.

"You don't have to stick around," I said to Moscow. "You know that, right?"

"I know, but I'm very curious to find out how your story ends. I have a good feeling about you." He gently smacked my cheek with his hand. "*The Book of Sam.* That could work."

We continued walking through the dry heat and the buzzing insects.

"Tell me something about your home. Anything, really," Moscow said. "I've never been to Berdym, but I see it in so much of my world, in clothing and in things powered by steam and horses."

His interest seemed genuine. To him, Berdym was some fantastical world of automobiles and sky-piercing towers, brought to life in stories told by merchants and slaves. I pictured all the different neighbourhoods and people of Toronto and riding the subway to get from one corner of the city to another. In every memory, Harper was right next to me.

"For my last birthday, Harper bought us theatre tickets. We dressed in nice clothes. Well, she did. She wore this green dress. Her mom told her it was only okay to wear it with me, 'cause I'm not like the other boys."

"She thought you were safe," Moscow said.

"I know. Anyway, I wore this old beige suit that didn't reach all the way down to my shoes. Also, a blue cummerbund that my uncle told me was all the rage. After the show, we just walked around the theatre district. I didn't want the night to end, but I also felt like we could be in that exact moment ten years later. Now, I don't even know if she's still alive."

We walked in silence, lost in the sky. Moscow kept removing his hat only to place it back on his head. Hollinshead and Thorlton were pretty far ahead of us.

"I miss her," I said. "I'm not a kid. I know that people die or go missing or run away, but it's different when it's someone you know."

Moscow looked at me. "It's different when it's someone you care about. If I learned one thing from living in a cell, it's that sometimes home isn't a place." He spat in his hand and extinguished his cigar.

"No, I guess sometimes it's not."

REGANSTRYFE

We didn't stop walking, not even for a short break, until we reached the top of a lush green hill. My brain refused to accept what my eyes were seeing on the other side, a scene that sent a chill down my spine. The hill overlooked a village frozen in horror, with the atmosphere of a crime scene. A dirt path snaked between wooden houses, all leaning into one another. The ground was covered with demons, their heads resting in dry pools of blood. Nothing moved unless manipulated by the wind.

"We're heading for the arch," Moscow said. At the edge of the town was an impressive black arch, its curved top looming over the landscape. In front was a swing carousel. The seats were high off the ground, attached to rusty chains fastened to a large blue-and-yellow half-moon hood. It reminded me of the one I used to ride every summer at the Canadian National Exhibition with my dad, one of the few good memories I have of him. It was a thrill, whipping through the air, waiting for one link of the chain to snap and cause you to fall to your death next to the Gravitron.

We walked past the ghastly faces with their eyes peeled open, blood pasted to the corners of their mouths.

"Should I even ask what's going on?" I said.

"Best to keep moving," Moscow said.

I jumped when a cold hand grabbed my ankle. A young demon was lying on her stomach, looking up at me, with some grass stuck to her face. The colour of the blood at the corner of her mouth deepened, returning to a more vibrant red.

She rose to her feet and dusted the dirt off her light-yellow polka-dot dress. She fixed her fire-truck red hair, patting it back into order.

"Welcome to Reganstryfe!" she said. "What brings you to town?"

I looked at a pile of bodies, waiting for the one on top to also rise and politely ask us questions.

"Oh, don't worry about them. They won't budge until the red equinox. I awake to welcome visitors."

She crouched down to Thorlton and scratched him behind the ears. The pleasure made his eyes roll into the back of his head.

"We're on our way to see Gary," Moscow said.

"The Leper Monk? Hmm, well, my name's Mandy. Could I interest you in a fresh-corn picnic in our meadow or a stay at our inn? Reganstryfe is also home to some interesting wildlife and vegetation, and you're in luck — we have room on our tour," she said. I felt like I was being worked over by a saleswoman from a rural tourism department.

"We're good," Hollinshead said.

She turned to me but pointed to Hollinshead. "What about some flowers for your lovely girlfriend?"

"Oh, no, we're not ..." Hollinshead said, trailing off in a rare display of insecurity. Her cheeks had turned bright red. Even though I couldn't see my own face, I had little doubt that I was blushing.

"Yeah, we're just, ya know ..." I added.

"I thought the same thing," Moscow said to Mandy, who nodded in agreement.

"Very well," Mandy said. "The colony is through the arches, but the other side is very dangerous. I will have Vlad escort you. He'll keep those on the other side at bay while you pass." She flashed a quirky smile. Her stare lingered for a few awkward seconds.

"The inn is having a special this week, free banana bread with ever—"

"Really, we're good," Hollinshead said, suddenly impatient.

"Very well. Wait by the arch and I will fetch Vlad for you. Please refrain from picking any flowers."

On our way to the arch, we stepped over several bodies that I was no longer convinced were dead, even though the stench suggested otherwise. We then waited for a long time.

Thorlton, Moscow, and I sat in a circle at the arch's base, surrounded by bright orange and blue tulips. Thorlton kept trying to pick the flowers but I grabbed his wrist and moved it away. He would huff and pout every time, before sneakily trying again.

Hollinshead leaned against the concrete arch, twirling a strand of her hair and looking in every direction. "I hope this Vlad guy actually shows," she said.

I wanted to talk to her about what had happened at Irekeep, but the timing didn't feel right.

A figure walked down the path. As he got closer, I could see that he was shirtless and wore a flowing purple cape over his grey skin, with a collar that reached high above his head. Something that looked like an old-fashioned gas mask covered his face, white discs blocking his eyes. A lantern dangled from his hand.

The demon, who we assumed was Vlad, stood nose to nose with Moscow and held the lantern right next to Moscow's head. He quickly shifted over to me and tilted his head as if trying to see something on the other side of my face. He did the same to Hollinshead and then to Thorlton. He pointed beyond the arch to a very normal-looking forest: dirt, trees, and leaves and the sound of small animals scurrying through brush, their claws digging into wood. There was nothing to arouse suspicion and no obvious need for a lantern.

Vlad approached the arch and raised the lantern high as he crossed the threshold.

"This forest belongs to the Alpsecords. Don't trust anything you see, and don't stop walking," Moscow said.

As soon as the four of us had crossed behind Vlad, the forest went black, as if someone had cut the power. I looked back and saw that Reganstryfe looked the same as it had only a moment before. Under the bright red sky were the carousel swing, the bodies, and the houses. In the middle of it all was Mandy, aggressively waving at us with a smile on her face. A smile that made me feel uneasy.

Half-formed shapes flitted in the darkness. Crisp leaves crackled underfoot, and dull growls came from somewhere behind me. Thorlton grabbed my hand, and I could feel his tremble. Mine trembled as well.

In front of us, I could see Vlad in the glow of his lantern, the bubble of light splitting the darkness of the forest. It was hypnotic to watch his cape float around him even though there was no wind here.

"She doesn't want you," a thin voice from the darkness said. I recognized that voice. It was Kyle's. But that was impossible.

"Did you guys hear that?" I said.

"Just keep following the lantern," Hollinshead replied. Her voice soothed my nerves — that is, until I felt hot breath on the back of my neck, forcing the hairs to stand up. I squeezed Thorlton's hand as tightly as I could.

A twig cracked. I spun around. Something was speeding toward me, its harsh scream gripping me between the conflicting instincts of fight and flight. After a second or two, it was almost right in front of me. Vlad ran over, whipped the lantern in front of my face, and illuminated a creature that walked on talons and had long ears that hung over its cluster of eyes. Two sharp fangs jabbed out of its closed mouth.

As the lantern's light moved closer to the creature, it cowered backwards, slinking away as if the light were a bullet spinning toward its head. It eventually retreated through the trees.

Vlad waved his finger disapprovingly in my face.

"He'll be good. Don't worry," Moscow said.

Vlad resumed leading us through the pitch-black woods. It was strange not to know where my next step would land. It was something I could never get used to.

"Sam," a soft voice whispered in my ear. "Why has it taken you so long? Why does it always take you so long?" Even though she sounded cold and sullen, I would have recognized that voice anywhere.

"Harper," I said, suddenly feeling lightheaded. All the strength left my legs.

"I don't have much time left," she said.

I turned around to see perforated edges in the darkness creating a faint outline in the shape of a young woman. It slowly faded away, as if the darkness were swallowing the weaker darkness.

"Sam. Sam. Let's go. C'mon," Thorlton said, unable to see what I was seeing. I had forgotten that I was still holding his hand. He pulled me forward, trying to catch up with Vlad, who was much farther ahead. "Go. Go. C'mon."

We walked for roughly another kilometre, and all I could think about was Harper. This whole time I had been chasing a memory through Hell, but I now realized something. A memory had also been chasing me.

The lantern revealed a white arch, telling us we had reached the end of the forest. Vlad turned to us, allowing me to finally see the others.

"I have brought you to the end of the Black Arch Forest. The colony is a short walk beyond the white arch," he said. "For this, you must present me with a gift."

"Like a gift card or something?" I said.

"Or something," Vlad replied.

Moscow reached into his pockets and took out the items he had stolen at the train station. He placed a clump of jewellery, a pocket watch, and a wallet in Vlad's cupped hands.

"This should do," Moscow said.

"Safe travels, and if you are ever in Reganstryfe again, please enjoy the fresh-corn picnic. Ask for Vlad."

As soon as we crossed through the arch, we were blinded by the natural light. I rubbed my eyes, waiting for them to adjust to the brightness.

"So now what?" I asked.

Thorlton was distracted by a scent. Hollinshead's eyes narrowed as she stared at a pile of branches next to a tree where a family of insects crawled up the trunk.

The branches rustled, and their leaves shook. They rose into the air, and suddenly there were spears and arrows pointed at our faces.

16
THE LEPER MONK

Sharp weapons were pointed at me from every direction. When I slowed down from exhaustion, one of our camouflaged abductors pushed a spear into my back, causing me to yelp. Moscow and Hollinshead were silent, walking with their heads down. Thorlton kept muttering and sniffing. I had no idea what was up with him.

"Sam. Sam. It's. It's. I think —" Thorlton said, but a strong poke cut off his rambling.

We walked single file along a path, weapons half-hidden all around us. I could see tips and hilts and a short guard tower covered by a light brown tarp.

Ash was smudged down our captors' cheeks, masking the one area of their faces that wasn't covered by the darkness of their hoods. Every so often they would mumble to one another. There was something about them I found familiar, but I couldn't put my finger on what it was exactly. More importantly, I couldn't figure out what they wanted from us.

A pair of wooden gates opened to welcome us. We entered an enormous clearing, surrounded by huts that were built right into the trees on three levels, the top level just below the treetops. Nature embraced this hidden community.

The huts sat on platforms supported by wooden beams that slanted toward the ground. The platforms were connected by a series of rickety bridges and catwalks constructed with wooden planks and bound together by rope.

We were brought to the centre of the clearing. My fear worsened as our captors formed a circle around us, their weapons drawn.

A hunched older demon with light-green skin walked down the staircase from the most elaborate hut, the one at the very top. He wore a dark-blue robe and had a bulbous nose and thick black horns. His right ear was missing and I counted only five fingers between his two hands. I was looking at one of the last Leper Monks in all of Hell.

Gary stood in front of us. He hacked uncontrollably, pounding his chest with his fist to clear the phlegm.

"I've been expecting you. Welcome to our little colony," he said in the gruffest voice I'd ever heard.

Moscow respectfully removed his hat and bowed. "It's an honour to meet you. My friend here is searching for someone and requires your unparalleled wisdom."

"Magpie will show you to my home and we can discuss it further," Gary said as he motioned for our captors to lower their weapons. They whipped off their hoods and removed their jackets. They were all Incubi, sharing the same features as Thorlton, except they were taller, stronger, more developed. Surrounded by his own kind, Thorlton was in a state of shock.

The colony inhabitants resumed their activities. Several females, who were called Succubi, walked in pairs with a staff spanning their shoulders and buckets of water dangling from it. A group of Incubi, cradling folded laundry, walked out of a hut, where steam smelling of hot detergent escaped from the chimney. On the side of the hut a stocky Succubus in a bloody apron stood at a large table, skinning the carcass of a long animal that looked like a four-legged snake.

"Sam! Sam!" Thorlton said, circling in excitement. He ran over to a mean-looking Incubus and poked him in the face, drawing a swat and a scowl. The Incubi all moved past him.

"Why are they ignoring him?" I asked.

"I can't figure one of them out, let alone a pack," Hollinshead said with a shrug.

Magpie was like Thorlton on Ritalin. He sported a handlebar moustache, and a long scar crossed his eye. We followed him up the tall staircase and into the Leper Monk's home.

Inside, a black curtain divided the room. The walls were bare except for one, where hooks were lined up to display rusty swords, one stained red. It reminded me of Cloaked Atlas and gave me a warm feeling, my first in a long time.

Gary stood next to a bookcase much like the one in my uncle's private collection. My eyes scanned the spines. *The Book of Camio*, *The Book of Gary*, *The Book of Dorian, The Book of Gutsmith, The Book of Dashiell, The Book of Ardat, The Book of Gorgora, The Book of Evelynn.* Only one book was missing.

"Magpie, get Philly, Crenshawe, Schmul, and the others to prepare some dinner for our guests. They'll be joining us," Gary said.

Gary stood before us, silent and rubbing his chin. The hunch of his back showed his age and made him seem burdened. He looked at each of us, appearing the most disappointed when he laid his eyes on me.

"Dorian and I have been using our considerable resources to keep track of you," Gary said.

Why didn't he stop us? I thought, but then remembered a point my uncle once made: the law of the Leper Monks forbids interference.

"Now, there is much to discuss," Gary said, sounding troubled.

"We're all ears," Hollinshead said, then cringed, avoiding eye contact with the demon missing an ear.

We followed him behind the curtain, which hid the ocular vein, a large stone vat holding a shallow pool of black water. This prized possession of the Leper Monks helped Evelynn and the Architects plan the precise moment to storm Belphegor, which led to the great city being taken. Moscow, Hollinshead, and I leaned on the edge of the vat, while Thorlton stood beside it, frustrated that he was too short to see what was going on.

"I cannot find Harper for you. I can only see those who rightfully belong to Hell," Gary said, slowly waving a hand over the black water.

"But as Moscow suggested on the train, I can tell you where Moloch is, and hopefully he can lead you to Harper."

"What's in it for you?" I asked.

"I sought help from my allies to capture Stolas before the situation could get worse, but every request I sent via my cipher was ignored or rejected. Which means, I'm afraid, that most are preparing to align with Stolas or surrender." He pointed a finger at me and Hollinshead. "The two of you brought Stolas back. Therefore, you need to rid our world of him once again. So much was sacrificed to sentence him to the mines."

Now I understood why he looked at me with such disappointment. Having me followed through Hell, he must have thought I was some great warrior. But here I was before him, a scrawny guy who peed his pants during his grade-six spelling bee instead of spelling *toboggan*.

I looked at Hollinshead and Moscow, hoping they were thinking the same thing I was: if this was the best deal, we were in serious trouble.

"My sources believe he's headed toward the Neeyson Valley in search of one of Alchem's Gift. There are rumours that the Demon Mother has one," Gary said.

Hollinshead perked up at the mention of another one of Alchem's Gifts. She knew that it presented another chance to return home, erasing my earlier mistake. "Why does he want one?" she asked.

"If history has taught us anything, it's that a demon who owns slaves can own a lot more," he said, then turned his attention only to me. "Sam, you understand that the consequences of this stretch to your world. There will be a thousand more Harpers taken and another thousand after that."

The gravity of the situation wasn't lost on me.

"Don't forget that Alchem's Gifts have other powers as well, powers that turned a throneless prince into an emperor," Moscow said, casting a pall over the room.

Gary made a fist above the black water and then splayed his fingers, issuing a command. We stepped back as the vat started to quake. He waved his hand as if conducting an orchestra. The water rushed to life, each drop part of a mosaic that depicted a scene like a translucent diorama. A watery Stolas walked through a burning village. The smoky smell with a hint of ash on the back of my tongue felt so real. He drew his sword as he stopped before a small helpless demon in stocks. The demon shook and cried. Stolas lifted his sword and hammered it on the back of the demon's neck. I watched him carry on through the village where those big and small, young and old, met the same fate.

The black water swirled, finally settling to tell a different story away from the horror of Stolas. In different parts of Hell — Anais, Mara, Beleth, Belphegor, Panthos — demons were amassing armies. The Krauss were sharpening spears on a whetstone. The Volacs were securing saddles on their serpents. The Alpsecords were smelting iron into the shape of arrowheads. It was the eve of war and all of Hell was preparing.

I felt guilty, knowing I had really screwed up. I had turned a search for my friend into events that could forever change two worlds.

"I will find Moloch for you. In exchange, you will return Stolas to the Banshees."

"We can't make that deal," I said. "What if Moloch doesn't know where she is, or what if we can't kill Stolas?"

"We have to," Hollinshead said. We all looked at her. "There's no other choice. The longer we wait, the less chance we have of finding her. And Moloch might have a way for us to get home. It's our only option."

Moscow nodded. They both looked at me as I gathered my thoughts. Against my better judgment, I agreed.

Gary walked to a chest and returned with four vials of water.

"Our pact will be consecrated on the River Styx. If you break it, you will all be sentenced on The Spear," Gary said. "There will be no running from our agreement."

He handed each of us a vial.

"One used to have to travel to the Styx to make these pacts, but now we simply drink its water."

We each unscrewed the top of our vial and drank the liquid. It tasted like normal water.

"*Antiqua praeconem mortuis per Infernum. Et consequatur erit adhaeserunt, ut,*" Gary said solemnly. Our pact was made. "Shall we find Moloch?"

Gary placed his face in his hands. I didn't understand what he was doing, and judging by her expression, neither did Hollinshead. His clawed fingers dug into his eyes, making a wet, squishy sound. His knuckles disappeared into his face as he grabbed hold of his eyeballs. He pulled them from their sockets and held them up for us to see. I watched in horror as they squirmed, moving around his palms as if they were motorized.

Hollinshead looked away. I couldn't hold back any-more, the knot in my stomach twisting so tight that I puked on the floor. Thorlton started to lick it up, but Moscow pulled him off. I looked at Gary, who now had two gaping black holes above a closed smile.

He placed his eyeballs in the vat, and they began swimming on small currents. The energized flow of water created hills, valleys, villages, and cities, a liquid version of Hell. The detail was incredible, drops of water lifting to form figures that filled the land. Belphegor rose to join the land, and in Mara, Hasha was wandering the streets drunk. Other figures moved in real time, walk-ing, sitting, drinking, eating, swinging axes, sharpening swords, fighting, kissing, playing, worshipping.

Gary whispered something in Latin, causing the water to swirl into what looked like the inside of the St. Lawrence Market back in Toronto.

"I see him," Gary said. He gave a quick wave over the vat, and the water became still.

"The Market of Midnight. That's where you will find Moloch." He picked up his eyeballs and popped them back inside their sockets. There was some resistance at first, but with a bit of force, he nuzzled them back in. Tears streamed down the creases on his face. I dry heaved. My stomach felt as if it would empty again at any second.

"Wash up, eat, and rest. I will have you escorted in the morning."

One day in grade nine, I sat alone in the cafeteria eating a semi-frozen beef patty. No one noticed me, which, truthfully, hurt as much as being picked on. Then Kyle sat across from me. He pretended not to see me, but as he started to eat his chicken burger, people at other tables looked over. More students filled the table, forcing me to the edge of the bench. The one next to me shifted again, pushing me onto the floor. I landed on my side as the room broke out in laughter. For weeks after, I ate in a bathroom stall. When Harper found out, she made me eat lunch with her every day in full view of the student body.

I realized that the more I missed Harper, the more my brain uncovered memories I hadn't thought about in years, memories I didn't even know were there.

A plate smashed on the ground, snapping me back to reality. On a platform high off the ground, we sat in a dimly lit mess hall. Thorlton and Hollinshead sat next to one another, across from Moscow and me. There were community tables full of fruit, lumpy oatmeal, chunks of bread, and fricassees of dark meat. I shovelled food into my mouth. It all tasted so good. A lot had changed since the "chicken" wings at Lady Baxter's Inn in Ragewick.

Thorlton slumped in his chair, his eyes moving all around the room. He had been oddly quiet during our time with Gary, and now he seemed even more distant.

"You all right?" I asked him, but got no reply. "Thorlton!"

I finally got his attention.

"How did you end up with Asag?"

"Sold. Sold to Asag. Thorlton too weak. Sold as baby," he said. I could tell he was getting upset. It upset me as well.

"What our friend here is trying to say is that in his kind, if one is too weak to perform, one is sold into slavery," Moscow said. He guzzled the rest of his Perry cider.

"Yeah, yeah. Asag told me," Thorlton said as Hollinshead put her arm around him.

We grew quiet. My thoughts drifted to the mission ahead of us.

"What should we do when we find Moloch?" I said, an eyebrow raised skeptically.

Hollinshead waved her fork. "Force him to tell us where Harper is."

"And if he doesn't want to?"

"I can be very persuasive," she said.

"And what about Stol—"

"There's always a way," Moscow said, cutting off my question. Probably a good idea, since there wasn't an answer.

Hollinshead must have noticed a shift in my demeanour. She looked at me like she was seeing me for the first time, without pity in her eyes and not on the cusp of some biting remark. I could never have anticipated what she was about to say.

"I've been in this world a long time and I've never met someone running around looking for their missing friend," she said. "I've seen demons beheaded, families sold into slavery or floating face down in a river, but no one's ever stopped me and said, 'Hey, have you seen my friend? I'm really worried about them.' That's not what this place is about."

"The wisdom of a Leper Monk," Moscow said, pointing at Hollinshead. She smiled at the compliment.

Behind Thorlton, Magpie arrived, his lip curled. Before I could ask what his problem was, he slammed his fist down on Thorlton's plate. The food exploded upon impact. Magpie then smacked Thorlton upside the head.

Moscow stepped up onto the table. The room went silent, the other diners glaring at us.

"My friends, there appears to be a bit of tension amongst the two camps here. We have only goodwill toward you, our new brothers and sisters. I know that Stolas is rather nasty business. As his former narrator and prisoner, I assure you I am well aware of what he is capable of. But I also know this: if there is one person fit to vanquish him, it is Sam. He might look young," Moscow stopped and crouched down to my ear. "How old are you?"

"Sixteen."

"Really? I would have guessed eight," he said as he straightened his body and smiled at the stone-faced crowd. "As I was saying, Sam is mature beyond his years and has journeyed from Berdym to become a bright new star in our world."

The demons went back to their meals, unimpressed with the speech. Moscow returned to his seat.

"Well, I tried," he said.

A Succubus wearing a blue dress, her head covered in a grey kerchief, cleaned up the shards and the spilled food. With a napkin, she wiped the mess from Thorlton's face and chest. She gave him a crooked smile and touched the tip of his nose before walking away.

After dinner, we tried to help clean up, but only Thorlton was allowed to pitch in. Hollinshead, Moscow, and I were ushered out without much explanation. We walked to the edge of the colony and sat on the dirt ground, each of us leaning against the side of a husky tree. Moscow struck a match and lit his cigar. After a minute, he began to loudly snore, the cigar clenched between his teeth.

I stared through the branches at the dark scarlet sky, feeling strange for some reason. I guess part of it was that this was the first time I'd ever had friends not named Harper.

When I looked down, I caught a glimpse of Hollinshead's wrist, the one with the scythe made of raised red skin. She noticed me staring, but instead of pulling her sleeve down, she rolled it up to her elbow.

"When I accepted Pazuzu's deal, he branded me," she said, the memory quivering through her.

I took her wrist in my hand. At first she tensed but then relaxed, letting me run my thumb over her mark. I was also starting to feel more relaxed in her presence, even though I was overwhelmed with questions about her life. I wanted to know everything about her, but I needed to confirm that the person who risked her life for me wasn't the same person who would help Pazuzu. I couldn't hold it in any longer.

"How could you do that to those people?" I asked.

"There's never been anyone running through Hell for *me*," she said, avoiding eye contact and hugging her knees tightly. "What choice did I have? Pazuzu kept wanting more and more. When I saw you in Beleth, I thought there might be another way."

Her honesty surprised me. Hollinshead was the type of person who would kill for you but get super annoyed if you asked her how it made her feel.

"The look on your face when you found out about me might have been the worst I've felt in a long time," she said.

"You would have brought Harper back to that guy."

"You're right." The openness of the moment seemed to take the wind out of her. She started to play with her hair. I mirrored her nervousness, stroking my own hair.

"You'll probably tell me to shut up, but I wanna know something," I said, bracing Hollinshead for the question I was determined to finally get an answer to. "How did you end up in Hell?"

She stared into the forest, her eyes vacant, lost in thought. She was silent for what seemed like an eternity. Maybe she hadn't heard the question.

"I was born on a farm in Virginia. It was just my dad and me. The farm hit rough times and he started drinking a lot, even more than this guy," she said, pointing to Moscow. "I was sitting on the porch one day when this woman from the bank walked up and handed me a letter. So I gave it to my dad, and he got really pissed off, even broke our coffee table. A few nights later, this man in a black fedora visited. I watched him from the top of the stairs as they sat in our dining room. My dad looked up at me — he knew I was watching the whole time."

I could tell she was gearing up to tell me the hard part. I gripped my knees, anxious.

"I woke up in the middle of the night, and when I went to close the window, I saw the man in the black fedora.

He was standing in our backyard, just smiling at me. All I wanted to do was find my dad, curl up in bed with him, and wait until morning. When I opened the door, the room filled with red fog. I guess you know the rest."

I struggled to find a response, something I could say to make her feel better.

"Your dad was a real douche," I said.

She smirked.

"I was a slave until I ran away and joined a mercenary group in Tower Hill. They taught me how to fight. Eventually, I ran away from them as well." She took a long, deliberate breath. "I've been running a long time."

Moscow fell over and started talking in his sleep. He was surprisingly still eloquent.

"I've never told anyone that story before," Hollinshead said.

"Most people don't tell me things," I said.

She let out a quick laugh and placed her hand on mine.

"I don't think my dad likes me," I said.

"Not the same thing, Sam, but thanks for trying."

That time we both laughed.

"Thanks for staying with me throughout all of this. Big thanks for not leaving me at Irekeep. Like, huge," I said.

"Your instincts suck," she said. "And you're a terrible judge of character."

I didn't want to wreck the moment by telling her she was wrong. Judging character was one of my few good qualities — Stolas being the exception, but hey, everyone gets one mulligan. I had known to stay away from

Kyle from the moment I saw how he enjoyed faking a punch just to make other kids flinch. Harper, on the other hand, I instantly labelled a keeper.

My mom taught me — or maybe it was Mr. Rogers — that if I was ever in trouble, I should look for a helper, because in every dangerous situation, there's at least one person who will help other people. I don't care how much she scoffed at the idea, Hell's helper was named Hollinshead — which still sounded Dutch to me.

Something about that moment pulled words out of mouth. I jumped right into telling Hollinshead about Kyle and my dad, about how small they made me feel. I talked about Harper, helping her understand why I had come to Hell. She just listened, not saying a word or pushing for details. When I finished, we sat in a silence that was anything but awkward. It felt comfortable, even nice.

"You guys are great," a semi-conscious Moscow said.

After a bit of time, Magpie came over and walked us to a small hut. The entire way I held Hollinshead's hand, our fingers interlocked. I lifted Moscow into a rickety hay bed and placed a blanket over him, as I would have with Uncle Bear. Hollinshead and I shared a bunk bed, me on the bottom. I didn't sleep a wink.

I got annoyed tossing and turning in the itchy hay, so I got up and went for a walk.

It was the middle of the night and the colony was much quieter now. I could hear insects chirping and something croaking. Thoughts of Harper turned in my head, memories of her face and the kind words she always managed to say. Those thoughts were usurped by harsher ones as I imagined her feeling lost and scared and even being in pain.

I followed faint voices to a hut on a crooked platform, connected to the ground by a couple of stone steps. Inside, it reeked of sweat. Thorlton, as animated as I'd ever seen him, was on a table in front of a seated crowd. His arms flailed about and words flew out of his mouth so fast that it was hard to make out what he was saying. I think he was doing an impression of me swinging Hollinshead's satchel at a Wanderer, and the crowd was eating it up. An Incubus slapped his knees as spit flew out of his mouth, making his black beard damp and stringy. A Succubus, the one who'd flirted with Thorlton at dinner, sat at the back staring at him lovingly.

I cleared my throat. All the beady and droopy eyes turned to me. Thorlton froze in mid-movement as if caught during a prison escape. Several of the demons walked over to me. A couple sniffed around my leg.

"Thorlton, I need to talk to you outside," I said, prying myself from the small crowd.

We sat on a log under a tree, and he told me all about his night. He was more at ease now. It was clear that being around his own kind agreed with him.

"Sam. Sam. What a night. So great. Great. They like Thorlton," he said.

"That's really good," I said. "Thorlton, can I ask you a question?"

He nodded and gave me his full attention.

"Why didn't you run away from the tavern in Mara? I mean, you could have taken the bolt out of your shackle and you knew a way out," I asked.

"Nowhere to go. No family."

His words broke my heart. I could no longer ignore a thought that had been nagging at me.

"You should stay here," I said, fighting against the words. He was caught off guard and jerked his head to look at me.

"I couldn't have made it this far without you, but you'll be safe here. If anything was to happen to you —"

"No, Sam. Find Harper," he said, his eyes welling with tears.

"I'll go with Hollinshead and Moscow. You deserve this. You'll be happy here."

"Thorlton and Sam! Why, Sam? Sam? Don't do it. C'mon. C'mon."

He rambled, arms crossed, petulantly looking away from me.

We sat in silence for a few minutes. I was trying to think of one good reason to take back what I'd said, but there wasn't one. Finally, I got up and walked away. He grabbed my pant leg, but I yanked it free. I didn't want him to see how much this hurt me. I knew this was best for him.

Magpie summoned Hollinshead, Moscow, and me to the most eastern corner of the colony. We stood under a white tarp held up by four metal poles. Swords and spears of different sizes leaned in stands next to woven baskets filled with arrows. I held a piece of chest armour that looked like it had survived many battles but was meant for someone shaped like an Incubus.

I then picked up a sword and a dented shield. For a moment, I felt like a knight, fearless and respected. Then I remembered that there wasn't a sword big enough to dupe anyone.

Outside the tent was a cannon sandwiched between two big wheels. One black cannonball was plunked in the grass beside it. The cannon looked so old, I wondered if it even still worked.

Gary stood on the other side of the tent, his hunched posture more pronounced than it had been the day before.

"Take what you need. Magpie will escort you to the market, and then my part of the pact will be complete," Gary said.

Hollinshead placed a sword in a scabbard on her back and a knife in the sheath attached to her ankle. Moscow refused to even touch a weapon, saying that he didn't believe in them.

With a shield on my back and a sword in a scabbard tied around my waist, I stood at the edge of the colony with Magpie and two other Incubi named Renoff and Michael.

Not far away, Hollinshead hugged Thorlton, and then Moscow gave him a stirring handshake and some words of encouragement. I wanted to say goodbye but couldn't bring myself to do it. He had truly given himself to my mission, and I couldn't stand the idea of being hated by him.

Magpie started hiking into the forest, and we all followed. I looked back at Thorlton, his eyes red and puffy. The Succubus, whose name I had learned was Ruthie, placed a piece of fur around his shoulders and rubbed his back.

Moscow pulled me by my arm. I turned my head once again. Thorlton was still looking at me. I gave him the smallest wave, and he returned the sentiment.

"You did the right thing," Magpie said. "You will go home or die, and then he would be alone. It's best he be with his kind."

"I know," I said. "Take care of him."

When I looked back one more time, the colony had blended into the forest, curtained by the wall of trees. I walked alongside Hollinshead and the cigar-chomping Moscow, behind three Incubi who all moved quickly with their heads down. Hollinshead seemed less present, her mind clearly elsewhere.

After some time, we approached a towering tree with an auburn trunk and branches full of colourful leaves. At the bottom, the trunk split to fashion an opening. Magpie pulled down one of the tree's boughs. The doorway magically lit up.

The tree's hollow interior was illuminated by a massive swarm of fireflies that darted above us, filling the space. They moved so fast, leaving trails of light and a warm radiance.

One firefly led the way, its stream of white light replacing the darkness. We made our way down a sloping tubular hallway that connected to an underground tunnel. I could see every grain of the wood, every ring etched on its curved walls. It smelled like pristine nature, fresh and untouched. I was amazed, but it was nothing compared to what was waiting for us on the other side.

THE MARKET OF MIDNIGHT

A charm of translucent finches flew above the market, gliding in circles that got smaller toward the centre, like a mobile spinning over a baby's crib. Their white light blanketed the market, which was as big as Ragewick, in a beautiful, bright glow.

I looked over hectares of space clogged by tents, tables, and exhibits. Hollinshead tapped my chest with the back of her hand.

"Let's get to work," she said.

We walked toward the entrance, where a demon stood on each side, their eyelids painted electric blue. They slid fiery torches into their mouths and breathed flames that crackled as they intersected over the doorway of the market.

"Sam, it's easy to get lost in this place, so stay close," Hollinshead said. "Also, don't buy anything."

We walked through a line of shouting merchants, whose volume didn't change based on crowd interest.

"Ash of Mara to keep your enemies at bay!"

"A bird's head to rid you of enemies! Maggots extra!"

"A Volac's ear to hear those you cannot see!"

"A bird's head to rid you of enemies! Maggots included!"

I found myself in the middle of the heavy traffic made up of every race of demon.

Raymond was right: Hell is an intersection of a hundred thousand worlds.

A large rat stood on his hind legs, testing lotions on his hairy arm.

Stay focused.

Wandering around this one alley was like touring a history museum. Moth-eaten togas and loincloths were displayed on headless mannequins. Next to them, whalebone corsets hung on a chain-link backdrop.

"Frames that hold only the memories you want to forget!"

"Stamps!"

A short card table in the front held monocles, white powdered wigs, and petticoats. Another stall displayed gold coins under a smudged glass case. Between two tables was a silver telescope, its lens pointed skyward.

All around me, reodes changed hands. Merchants waved away demons offering only a circle of copper or tin.

When we turned into the next alley, I was hit by a pungent smell. I walked over to some stacked barrels that were alternately filled with nuts and spices.

A young demon with small eyes and a tiny nose sidled up beside me. He flashed a smile, revealing a space between his two front teeth. He took my hand and dropped a handful of a yellow-tinged spice into my palm. It was cold and silky as it sifted through my fingers. Hollinshead whistled at me. I thanked him and left to join the others.

"This place is huge, so we need to split up," Hollinshead said. "I'll go with Sam and Renoff. Michael and Magpie, you guys stay with Moscow."

It felt like one of those let's-all-put-a-hand-in-the-middle-for-a-team-cheer moments, but I resisted. We broke off into two groups. Hollinshead and I headed down an alley with Renoff trailing behind.

Tables separated by curtain walls were filled with more modern items: skateboards, scooters, books, and smartphones. Farther ahead were wallets, clothing, shoes, boots, purses, jewellery, and baseball caps, all of which looked like they could be bought at any department store. Hollinshead sensed my confusion.

"When someone's brought to Hell, everything they have is taken and sold here."

"That's awful," I said, looking at a rack of tattered dresses. I picked up a Yankees cap and noted the dried blood stuck to the rim. I was overwhelmed by everything. All these people taken from their homes and someone left wondering what had happened to them. My uncle never told me about this place. Now that I think about it, he always danced around the parts that showed Hell's coldness.

I stopped at a table to look at a sea of wallet-sized photos that seemed to span the history of photography. I saw scenes of friends and families and some of children posing or playing. One featured two young boys arm in arm in front of a funhouse. Another captured a little girl, no more than five, and a small terrier. She was running through a bright-green field on a summer's day, carrying a Nerf football, a big smile on her face. I only stopped staring at it when Hollinshead barked at me to keep moving.

At the end of the alley was a fortune-telling Alpsecord, a fez tilted like a crown on his head. He reminded me of Todmorden, an Alpsecordian farmer who suffered from premonitions. In the story, he sailed for weeks down the Gwyn River to warn demons who lived on The Spear about the construction of the Mines of Belphegor.

"Ever hear the story of Todmorden?" I asked.

Hollinshead sighed, signalling that she wasn't interested in hearing more.

"What is it about this world you love so much?" she asked.

"I think my uncle told me these stories to show me that there was adventure and heroes and things worth fighting for, but maybe also to help me escape," I said. "That's the point of stories, right?"

"I guess. I'm not interested in discovering more. I'm interested, though, in things like …" She thought for a moment. "Have the Orioles won the World Series recently?"

"No."

"Anything new with cars?"

"Some are driverless."

"Shut up!"

"It's true."

"Tell me more."

I had never held her attention like I did in that moment. As we strolled through the market, I got her caught up, as best I could, on pop culture, politics, and recent World Series champions. I even tried explaining things like Instagram and Snapchat. She seemed the most excited about Star Wars and the least excited about the Brangelina breakup. I had trouble matching her excitement, though. Since our conversation the night before, my confused feelings about Hollinshead were becoming clearer.

"So what are you going to do if you make it home?" I asked.

"I haven't even thought that far. In case you haven't noticed, I've been a little busy."

"C'mon, you can't tell me you've never thought about it."

She stared at her feet, maybe hoping the answer was hidden on her boots. A warm smile crossed her face.

"I guess I'll do everything I should have done: have a chat with my dad, burn his farm down, maybe go to school, get a job, get fired, catch a ballgame, the usual. What about you?"

"What about me?"

"Things will be different for you, Sam. You'll have Harper and you won't be such a dork anymore."

"Maybe," I said, struck by her point.

All of a sudden, Hollinshead swooped in front of me, stopping me in my tracks. "Listen, thanks for last night. I shouldn't have been so cold to you before."

"I should be thanking you. You could have walked away from this a long time ago, especially after the whole box thing," I said, taking her hand in mine. In that moment, the noise of the market dimmed.

"You talk too much."

"Only when I'm nervous," I said. "I'm always nervous."

Hollinshead blushed. I finally saw her as the lost teenaged girl who had been ripped from her home, not the hardened warrior who had fought and killed her way to this market, or the survivalist who would drag slaves back to their unrightful owner. She stared into my eyes, delivering to me a surge of confidence that I had never experienced before. Of course, my newfound confidence didn't prevent sweat from pouring out of my body at a record pace. I pushed aside some hair that fell in front of her face. She closed her eyes and slowly leaned in.

Before our lips touched, I saw something over her shoulder, something that tightened my stomach and chest. A stark reminder of where I was. My heart swelled.

A light-green hoodie hung on display behind a table, the arms spread wide, the hood shredded, a splatter of red down the middle.

MOLOCH THE TRICKSTER

"We should get Moscow," I said, deflated, unable to take my eyes off Harper's hoodie. The sight of it brought up a memory that I badly wanted buried.

Hollinshead rubbed the back of her neck and awkwardly looked everywhere but at me. I waved for Renoff to come over.

"No, if you're sure that's her hoodie, then let's go have a chat," she finally replied. She reached down to remove the knife from her ankle sheath.

We waited for a family of Volacs to go by and then walked to the stall, the merchant's eyes boring into us. She had the lower body of a goat and the upper body of a haggard woman. Her long, ratty hair covered some of the warts on her face.

"We're looking for Moloch," I said.

The woman unfurled her forked tongue, and as she hissed, spit landed on my face. "East end of the market, near the booksellers. The grey tent," she said.

We thanked her and followed her directions.

The booksellers were a group of old demons with wrinkly skin, beady eyes, and grey hair that looked fried. Skin hung off their faces like dripping wax. Four of them fumbled through stacks of books double their height, obsessively dusting and inspecting each one. A couple of others used quills to write on catalogue cards, which they handed to the oldest-looking one, who organized them in the long drawer of a cabinet.

Connected by brass brackets was a row of tall book-cases, the sides shaped like thick beanstalks and holding up shelves of different lengths. A bookseller, halfway up a ladder on wheels, used his hands to push off and rocket from one end to the other. He picked out certain books and tossed them to his colleagues below.

Over the tops of the other stalls, we could see a grey nylon tent held up by poles. Hollinshead followed me down a tight alley. Bright graffiti on the wall read "The Path of the Curious." It felt like a warning. Either way, a lump formed in my throat as we approached an opening with a sign.

BEWARE: PURVEYOR OF AUTHENTIC GOODS

"This is it," I said.

The closer we got, the more skittish Renoff became. I told him to wait for us and we left him there in the alley.

Inside the tent, a lantern gleamed on a table, the diffused light casting our shadows on the walls. A wooden chair was pulled out from the table, and a black screen cut off a corner of the tent. Behind it, a grainy male voice repeated, "Spirits of the past, visit upon us. Spirits of the past, visit upon us. Spirits of the past, visit upon us."

I slowly walked behind the screen and found a phonograph spinning a vinyl record. I lifted the needle and the voice disappeared.

"Not a fan of parlour tricks?" someone said.

I stepped out from the behind the screen and was startled to see that the chair that had been empty a moment before now had someone in it: a Hanbi in a black fedora. He was happy to see us.

"I should get some credit for this, should I not?" he asked, moving his finger back and forth between Hollinshead and me.

Hollinshead stared at him, stunned. He leaned back with his hands steepled on his stomach. I was now looking at the real Maurice Locke, a Hanbi, although still dressed in a suit featuring a perfectly folded pocket square.

"That record, along with a boom in Ouija boards, once made my job much easier. These days, I must resort to business deals. It's always about finding that right person: a man so scared to lose everything he owns or an insecure young man who just can't tell a girl how he feels," Moloch said. "The funny thing with you, Sam, is I just pointed you in the right direction, and you did the rest."

I really hated this guy.

"Shirley here was different. I had to be very persuasive with her father," he said.

I looked at Hollinshead and mouthed, "Shirley?"

Hollinshead didn't acknowledge me or what Moloch had just said. She looked broken by his words.

"The sad thing is he lost the farm a few years later. Tough economy or something."

She made a fist. I gently grabbed her wrist to make sure she didn't lunge at Moloch and rip his head off.

"Where's Harper?" I asked.

"She was delivered to her owner."

"And who would that be?" Hollinshead said.

"It doesn't matter at this point." He got up and walked over to the phonograph and placed his finger-nail on the vinyl. After a moment, it started to spin. The tent filled with the sound of a violin concerto. He turned and faced us; the music continued to play.

"It wasn't personal. I answer to someone whose wish is for certain possessions from Berdym. In exchange, I get more time there. I love Berdym — the women, the food, the filthy air, everything."

Hollinshead pushed him against the wall and kneed him in the groin. He bent over, wincing. She pushed him back up, her hand gripping his neck.

"You already got paid. In fact, finding her will prob-ably get us killed, so you have nothing to lose."

He struggled against Hollinshead's grip. I moved closer and placed the tip of my sword on his thigh. I pushed it into his flesh. I couldn't believe how easy this was. Any hesitation I felt was overridden by the need to hurt him.

He was in obvious pain. Hollinshead looked at me with surprise.

"She was sold to the Demon Mother," Moloch blurted out between deep breaths.

"Abyzou," I said.

Hollinshead backed up, two fingers covering her mouth. I could tell that she knew as well as I did that this wasn't the answer we wanted to hear.

"The Demon Mother doesn't like to lose her children," Moloch said. "Just ask Stolas."

Hollinshead looked at me with fear in her eyes but then turned back to Moloch.

"Do you have a way for us to get home?" she said.

"I left the box with Sam because I didn't want to return to Hell. My hope was that the girl was enough to buy my freedom. But my debts proved too large, so the fog came for me," he said. He looked to the side as he searched his brain. "Abyzou might have another, maybe some traders. These items are scarce and change hands fast. Even the Hanbi have run out. It's possible there's no way back."

Hollinshead looked as if a small part of her had died. I put my hand on her shoulder to comfort her.

A commotion outside stunned us into silence. Wordless cries drowned out by squawking and thumping. The faint smell of smoke. As our attention focused on the tent's opening and whatever was happening in the market, the roof split open and a bloody finch fell next to our feet.

We ran through the alley, stopping just before the rows of burning stalls. Under the pall of smoke, stalls were collapsing, eaten by fire. Dead finches were scattered across the ground and more twirled on their way down, feathers floating through the sky. A committee of vultures with bald faces and black-feathered bodies tore the wings off the small birds, and every time they were successful, the market grew darker.

The market was in frenzy. Tables were being toppled as a cacophony of screams came from all directions. Demons and creatures scattered like roaches, hoping to get as far away as possible. Several got trampled under the growing din of the frightened crowd.

Eyes stared at me but couldn't see me. They couldn't see anything anymore. I remained frozen on the sidelines of the chaos.

"What's happening?" I asked.

I found the source of the panic. Pazuzu stood in front of a group of Hanbi who were as still as statues, their arms crossed in front.

Pazuzu's bones snapped, elongated, and then moved back into place. His torso lengthened like taffy as his spine ruptured through the skin of his back, and his fingers sharpened into claws. The red glow from his eyes spread to the middle of his face, filling the slivers in his broken skin. He had become the monster we had seen during our escape from Beleth.

The area was now clear; everyone had either left or been killed. Renoff appeared out of nowhere, running toward Pazuzu with his sword drawn. He was no match, though, as Pazuzu plunged his claws into the top of his head.

Another death, all because of me.

"We need to run," Hollinshead shouted over the noise. She scanned the area looking for a way out, but couldn't find one. Hanbi were scouring the grounds.

"Where? There's nowhere to go and we can't leave Moscow," I said. "I'll distract him."

"Yeah, right," Hollinshead scoffed. "Wait here, I'll handle this."

As she moved to step out of the alley, I grabbed her arm, but she pulled away and then ran off and disappeared behind some stalls. I crouched lower, trying to blend into the wall, surrounded by screaming and death. There was no shelter from it, no way to feel safe amid everything that was happening. I was hidden for only a minute before a strong hand grabbed the back of my neck and dragged me into the alley. It was a Hanbi, one who looked quite proud of himself.

When Pazuzu saw me, his mouth curled into a smile. A Hanbi kicked the back of my leg, forcing me to one knee. My shield and sword were removed and thrown behind us. The Hanbi moved to the side of the alley. I was being prepared for execution.

Everything moved fast. I heard a smack and a grunt. I looked over to find the Hanbi who had captured me lying on his side, a dribble of blood on his scalp, with Magpie and Michael standing over him. Pazuzu lowered his body, puffed out his chest, and unleashed a wrath of fire. My heart quickened as I dropped my head and crossed my arms in front of me. But before the flames could touch my skin, a barrier appeared before me, diverting the fire into two streams and preventing me from being burned to a crisp.

Moscow stood in front of me, his head down, his arm in the straps of my shield. Smoke and heat turned the small triangle of space into a makeshift oven.

Moscow shuffled his feet, pushing against the fire's fury.

A spear spiralled through the air, piercing Moscow between his shoulder blades. He grunted as his arms opened and he dropped to his knees. The shield fell to his side. The fire continued to blaze, wrapping around Moscow's body. Charred bits of flesh floated into the air as he fell to the ground. Seconds later, the fire started to run out of fuel. I crawled backwards trying to distance myself from the dying flame.

I looked over my shoulder to see who had thrown the spear. On the roof of a nearby exhibit was Stolas, smiling at the corpse of his former narrator. Magpie and Michael appeared on the roof behind him, swords drawn. It took a moment for Michael to make the first move, swinging his sword hard, only to have it blocked by the padding on Stolas's wrist. In one swift motion, Stolas ended Michael's life with a stab to the gut. Magpie stepped forward to take his turn.

I had to stop watching them and return to my situation. The fire had ceased and the alley had grown quiet. It was just me and Pazuzu on the ground. He readied himself to release another blast of fire, delivering me to the same fate as Moscow. But the fire petered out into smoke as he tried to blow. He fell face first to the ground, half of a sword sticking out of his back and blood staining his robe. Gripping the handle of the sword was Hollinshead, three dead Hanbi behind her. She leaned over Pazuzu in exhaustion.

I looked at Moscow's teeth, the only part of him that wasn't burned beyond recognition, but had to turn away. It was too hard.

Something rolled toward me, stopping when it hit my forearm. It was Magpie's head, frozen in fear. I could barely breathe. Anxiety made my body feel like a champagne bottle about to pop.

Stolas jumped down and strode toward me. As he got closer, I could see that his eye was seared closed and blistered. I crawled backwards some more, trying to escape, but there was nowhere to go.

Hollinshead removed her sword from Pazuzu's flesh and ran toward Stolas. When she was close enough, she tried to slice him across the chest, but Stolas leaned out of the way. She followed with more jabs and strikes but was overpowered. Stolas knocked the sword out of her hand. With his other hand he grabbed her throat, lifting her off the ground. The pressure of his squeeze might have killed her, but instead, he dropped her onto a pile of corpses and broken wood. He was concerned only with me.

I scampered on my hands and feet toward Hollinshead's sword, but before I could reach it, Stolas pushed me to the ground, his boot on my back. He flipped me over with his foot.

"I paid a visit to an old friend and his little colony. Found these useful in finding you," Stolas said as he dropped two cloudy eyeballs onto my stomach. I knew they were Gary's by the way they squirmed like frightened mice. My thoughts shifted to Thorlton.

Stolas reached over and pulled the spear out of Moscow's back. His boot on my chest kept me in place. Hollinshead climbed out of the rubble, trying her best to draw his attention away from me, but her voice and body were too broken.

I couldn't take my eyes off the sharp point aimed at my gut. My jaw was sore from clenching.

He thrust the spear down, spiking it into my stomach. It tore through skin and tissue. My body jerked up, blood poured out of the wound, and tears fell from my eyes. A twist of the spear sent jolts of pain to every part of my body. Blood rose through my throat, choking me. My heart slowed, every beat feeling like it would be the last. I looked at his ghostly smile and the red sky above, where finches continued to meet their demise. Flashes in the corner of my eye spread across my vision. Then the world began to grow dark.

Hollinshead fell to her knees. Tears moistened her cheeks.

Her face was the last thing I saw.

THE NOTHINGNESS

Hell is an intersection of a hundred thousand worlds. There was one exception, though, one world that could never intersect with another. The Nothingness existed beyond the physical, a place where the mind could go but the body was forbidden. It was an ether fuelled by the nightmares of the Alpsecords. They called it home until they were driven out by a plague that cut their population in half.

No air filled my lungs. No sounds rang in my ears. Despite this, I still felt a heavy presence as I floated through black space. What that presence was, though, was impossible to say. I know this makes no sense, but give me a break — I was floating through nothing.

A voice said, "Nothingness. Make choice. Very bad, Sam. The other place. Very bad." I couldn't put a face to that voice. Coldness grew in my heart. The voice was suffocated by hundreds of whispers that came together like a deafening klaxon.

Near my feet, the black rippled, small bubbles forming along its surface. The bubbles stretched into thin, nimble fingers. Hands rose out of the gel-like blackness and wrapped around my wrists and ankles and under my chin, slowly tightening like the grip of a vise. With one violent tug, they pulled my shoulders out of their sockets, separated my legs from my hips, and detached my head from my neck.

In that moment, I welcomed death.

The black swirled, opening a small hole before me, allowing a cone of light in. I wanted to shield my eyes from it, but my arms had floated away. All I could do was squint and panic. The whispers ceased.

"You get one chance," said an ominous baritone voice that travelled through the hole. "If you choose to take it, it will be decided if you can return. If you decline, you will move on to the next world."

I screamed in agony.

"Silence," the voice demanded, reprimanding me for acknowledging my pain.

My eyelids stretched down each side of my nose and over my lips to cover my mouth. My face became a fleshy blank canvas. The thought of what was happening to me was as horrifying as the intense pain.

"You can wait and receive visits. At some point during the visits, the sole star will flicker twice and you will then be weighed. If you choose not to wait, you will be sent to the next world. Before you decide, know this: it has been written that you will find peace in the next world, but choosing the other path will change that."

My head drifted down the endless shimmering black landscape. My heart was beating out of control inside my chest, which hovered above me.

"I will await your decision," the voice said. The pain took hold of my brain and, even though the sound couldn't leave my mouth, I screamed until my throat was raw. It consumed me.

A barrage of images flashed in my mind, but the figures that appeared weren't nameless, their voices weren't faceless. It started with my first memory of school, when my mom used a frog puppet to lure me inside the classroom. It shifted to Uncle Bear, a decade younger than he was now, and a sleepover at Cloaked Atlas, where we were reading a chapter from *The Book of Dashiell* together. I thought of Harper, Hollinshead, and Thorlton, and of Moscow's corpse after he died protecting me. In between each was the image of me naked in the locker room, deflating under the sound of laughter. I thought of Stolas.

These faces lingered until, once again, details about who they were slowly flitted away. No matter how hard I tried, and I really did try, I couldn't remember them. I searched every corner of my mind for clues, but I kept coming up empty. I refused to let go of the images, forcing them to stay clear in my mind for as long as possible.

"Your decision has been made," the voice said.

The skin over my mouth separated and crawled back up my face until it was just my eyelids again. I blinked several times, feeling the smallest sense of relief.

The space in front of me dissolved into a fog, revealing the outline of a face. The fog lifted and Moscow materialized. It felt good to see him. We were in the rubble of the market. It smelled of death, with warm notes of the pungent spices that filled the barrels.

I ran my hand all over my arms and legs and felt around my mouth. I was whole again, but I didn't know if this was real or not.

In the normally featureless sky, a lonely star shone yellow against the ceaseless red. Moscow stood over his charred remains, his hands in his pockets. I waited for him to show a glimpse of his typical light mood and personality. But he just stood there, morose.

I turned to see my own body impaled by a spear, lying in a dry pool of blood. It was horrifying to see my own corpse frozen in the way in which it was murdered. I barely recognized myself.

"I'm sorry I got you killed," I said.

Moscow's reply was to light his cigar.

We walked through the wreckage of dead bodies and destroyed stalls, the ground littered with merchandise. Fire had reduced much of the market to ash. It felt as if I were walking through a battlefield the day after the battle had ended. I had seen death before but had never felt it so strongly in my bones.

"You caused all of this," Moscow said.

I looked over at a pile of bodies. Even though the one on top was headless, I knew it was Moloch from the straight edge of his pocket square.

"Was Harper worth this? Does all this justify your cause?" he said. I didn't have an answer, or at least not one I wanted to acknowledge.

We finally stopped in front of a wooden table, a pair of black boots sticking out from underneath it. He lifted the table, confirming my fear. I dropped to my knees in front of Hollinshead and buried my face in her cold stomach. Her lips were blue, a streak of blood ran down one side of her face, and the other side was scorched and raw. I lost it and started to cry uncontrollably.

"She didn't last long against Stolas. Thorlton was killed in the raid at the colony, and … well, you know what happened to me. Others came to stop him and met the same fate."

I remembered what the market was like when we first arrived. How it brimmed with life, energy, and wonder.

Moscow stared at me with dead eyes. Even though he was right in front of me, I missed him and wished the real Moscow were here. This Moscow pointed to the spinning yellow star in the sky. It flickered once and, like a curtain falling, the scenery changed. I now found myself standing in Cloaked Atlas on a rainy night. It felt safe — for a moment, it felt like home.

Uncle Bear gazed out the window. A streetcar created fat sparks along a cable as it barrelled down a spectral Spadina Avenue. The streets were empty, and the shops and restaurants were dark. Above the skyline was a sea of stars. One shone brighter than the rest.

"I failed you," Uncle Bear said, except he didn't sound like my uncle. Iciness had replaced his usual charm, and even the glimmer in his eyes was gone. "Filling your head with stories of heroes and adventures. I thought you were like me when I was your age, craving something bigger and wanting to experience everything. I was wrong."

Lightning crashed, filling the room with a thunderous boom. I stood next to Uncle Bear; his ice-cold hand grabbed mine.

"You should have chosen the next life, Sam. It would have been peaceful for you. You've changed what will happen to you if you die again — if you even get the chance." He let go of my hand and wheeled himself to the counter, which was shrouded in darkness.

I waited for the star to flicker, hoping that this moment would end, but its brightness held without interruption. I thought I had achieved so much, but he was right: my quest to find Harper had ended the same way as everything else I'd ever done.

"When you were a boy, you wanted to do so many things, but you always failed. Me, your father, teachers, other kids in school, their parents, we all felt sorry for you. We kept hoping that some young men just mature late."

His words stung and made me think of the basement in our house, which was a monument to how bad I was at a lot of things. There was a hockey bag next to a guitar, which was next to a pile of golf clubs, baseball bats, chess pieces, computer parts, paintbrushes, and dance shoes.

A loud snap made me jump. Uncle Bear's head slumped, and his arms went slack by the side of his chair. I called to him but got no response. He disappeared into the shadows.

In his place, a smile broke through the darkness. My dad's dimpled chin and thin eyebrows were unmistakable. Then a shadow swam across his face, rearranging his features and smile into Kyle's. His stare lingered, broken only when another shadow danced across his skin, hiding him from my view. Cloaked Atlas, the only place that ever felt like home, had become a zoetrope, holding and projecting my deepest fears. I knew who was next.

Movement in the shadows broke the eerie calm of the room. Stolas stepped toward me, wielding a blood-stained spear. His jaw lowered, releasing a shrill scream. He hurled the spear. It spun tightly as it flew toward me, and then it broke through my stomach and emerged from my back, splattering blood on the floor. The pain was worse than the first time. I stumbled into the window, my hands leaving red prints on the glass.

On the street, blood oozed through sewer grates and was washed away by waves of more blood that whooshed along Spadina. The current carried dead bodies, all those who had died in the wake of my failure. The floor felt like it was moving underneath my feet.

The star flickered and I fell through the floor and landed in my school cafeteria. The bloody wound on my stomach was gone, leaving only a small hole in my shirt. I tried to calm myself, but I couldn't catch my breath.

Students walked around me carrying fried food on plastic brown trays. The long orange tables were filled with teenagers, most of whom I recognized. I saw Dale Hammersmith's freckled face shooting spitballs at the back of Warren Browning's head. The tallest girl in my grade, Dayna Mantook, looked annoyed as she tried to tutor the Chrises (as they had been called since middle school): Chris Blatt, Chris Maclean, and Chris Howe.

Jeremiah Cormac and Jason Chu sat at a table wearing their mustard-coloured hockey jerseys, each with an arm around one of the Turner sisters. On the far side of the room, Madison Case was clearly breaking up with Rob Jacobs, our disgraced school president who was impeached for stealing from the treasury. He wasn't taking it well and kept trying to hold her hand. In a corner, Mitchell Roth sat alone playing a game on his laptop, his head snuggled into a big pair of headphones. Attached to the wall near the double doors was a big gold star cut out of construction paper.

I kept searching the room, knowing that she had to be there somewhere. I lifted myself to the tips of my toes, trying to see the far corner, where a cluster of students pointed at me while laughing at something on their phones.

From behind me a soft voice, the same one I'd heard in the Black Arch Forest, said, "Sam."

I turned around and there she was, sitting at a circular table, her legs crossed at the ankles. She bit into a sandwich, then took a sip of Diet Coke through a straw. I sat across from her, wanting to hug her, but this wasn't a reunion.

"I miss you," Harper said, her face warped by a fake smile.

"I miss you, too."

"Still making me say things first," she said.

I paused to collect my thoughts. Even with this Harper, I was having trouble taking that leap.

"That night, I was going to tell you that I love you," I said, even though it was painful to admit. "What happened to you? Are you still alive?" I stuttered the last question, unable to stop my voice from cracking.

"Doesn't matter. It's too late, Sam."

I lowered my head, not wanting to admit that I had failed. She took another bite of her sandwich. Her mannerisms and scent were exactly as I remembered them, but she was cold and emotionless.

"You have nice memories of me," she said.

"Yeah. Do you have any of me?"

"Of course I do. I have memories of us. I remember you egging Spencer Washington's house after he kissed Megan Kowolo even though he'd asked me to the semi-formal. I remember your dad yelling at you for getting cast as a bush in the school play. I remember when we were kids and I was crying so you stuck an eraser up your nose to make me laugh."

"I remember you waiting in the emergency room with me until the doctor removed the eraser," I said.

Her smile dropped like an axe, and her tone shifted. "I also remember you hiding from Kyle and the look on your face when I showed you those pics," she said.

Her memory reminded me that not long ago I had been hiding again, in an alley, waiting for Hollinshead to save the day, hoping the storm would pass.

Harper pushed half of her sandwich over to me. It was two slices of white bread stuck together by a thin layer of gloopy peanut butter.

"What's with that other girl, Sam?" she asked. "Do you miss her like you miss me?"

Suddenly I was in the hot seat, trying to dodge suspicion.

"I don't know. It's really confusing."

"You've always been easy to read," she said, tilting her head, trying to find my eyes, which were aimed at the table. "It's hard for me to picture you and her together. I waited years for you."

I ignored her comments about Hollinshead. I already felt torn apart by a maelstrom of feelings, and thinking about her only made it worse.

"So what's going to happen to you?" I asked.

"Whatever the Demon Mother wishes," Harper said. A deep, deliberate breath followed her words, and when it was done, her face grew sad.

My eyes were drawn to her neck. She was wearing the necklace I had given her, the one with the broken clasp. A thought hit me hard — so hard, in fact, that it struck like thunder. My memory brought me back to the night Harper was taken, the now-destroyed box in my hands, the still-alive Maurice before me. I had been so focused on the box, forgetting that it held an item, a piece of jewellery. Maybe I was searching for something that wasn't there, or maybe I never really stopped to think about it, focused as I was on my mission. But there was a chance that, like the box, the necklace was one of Alchem's Gifts. If it was, then it could be my ticket home. That is, if I could get out of the Nothingness and if I could find it — big ifs. I racked my brain trying to remember what Harper had done with it, but my memory seemed to jump from her holding the necklace to her being dragged away. Still, this was a win. Sort of.

The last person I was hoping to run into in this cafeteria arrived. Kyle stood behind Harper, his hand cupping her shoulder. He looked at me with the same expression of disgust he'd had since kindergarten.

The doors to the cafeteria burst open. I stood up as everyone else continued with what they were doing. Harper looked as if she had accepted her fate. It made me feel pathetic for trying to save her, for chasing her memory through Hell.

"Don't fight it," she said solemnly as Kyle walked her to the doors.

I looked at the cut-out star and it flickered once. Then a few seconds later it flickered again. The walls of the room pushed out, the floor dropped, and once everything settled, I was standing on a circular marble platform. There was no ceiling or walls. Only a refreshing sky surrounded me. I had grown so used to the red sky of Hell that it was weird to see a blue one streaked with white.

A tall demon with bushy red hair and angular eyes leaned on a cream-coloured standing scale, the kind where you had to slide black blocks along numbered bars to determine your weight. Next to him was a short, fat demon with large ears.

"Welcome, Sam!" the tall one said, his arms stretched out to welcome me. "I am Dorian, and this is my assistant, Fenimore."

The Book of Dorian. Dorian was an Arkavelle. It was his baritone voice that had interrogated me in the black of the Nothingness. By trade he was a noble statesman, but by legacy he was one of the Architects, a close companion of Gary, Evelynn, and Dashiell. From what I had learned from Moscow, he was betrayed by Stolas and forced into hiding. The Architects were proof that nothing good ever came from trying to save others.

Fenimore made me stand on the old-fashioned scale.

"This scale was a gift from a Berdymian trader to Mara, queen of the Alpsecords," Dorian said. He slid a black block all the way to one side, then inched it back and forth, trying to decipher what the scale was telling him. "She knew that nightmares come from one's deepest fears and that, like all emotions, fear carries a weight. It has substance. The true gift of the Alpsecords wasn't their talent for crafting nightmares. It was their ability to weigh fear against hope."

Dorian looked intently at the numbers, seeming to crunch them in his head.

"So what are you looking for?" I said.

"Let's just say it's something with an exact weight. This scale, and only this scale, can weigh it. If it is present, then you're in luck. If not, well, we'll discuss that if we need to," he said. "Step off, please."

I stepped back onto the platform as Dorian and Fenimore huddled nearby. Dorian kneeled down and whispered into Fenimore's ear. Fenimore nodded. Dorian rose to his feet, and they both looked at me.

"You think of her often."

I was struck by his statement.

"If you dig deeper into a memory you can find something else — regret, happiness, guilt, sadness, pain, love, a combination of these. They can remain or simply drift away. But with you, there is a weight and that weight is heavy."

"So?" I asked.

"So, per the Law of Mara, the first settler, it is a reason to be given a second chance," Dorian said. "The Alpsecords aren't monsters, as history has painted them to be. They believe that emotion is one's true nature and that all beings should be rewarded based on their nature. They are a complicated race, but not heartless."

None of this made sense to me, but I was beyond the point of trying to make sense of everything in this world. Dorian stepped toward me and placed his hands on my shoulders.

"Sam, the scale has found that you have what is required."

We walked to the edge of the platform. Nothing but clear sky below.

"This is a glorious opportunity, but it is a one-time deal. If you die again in Hell, only the negative is weighed against you. There will be nothing you can do."

We stood at the edge of the platform, the heels of my shoes hanging over.

"When you arrive, an escort will be waiting to guide you to one place of your choosing. Whatever you do, do not sign up for the fresh-corn picnic. It's overpriced for tourists."

"Oh, that guy," I said.

"Don't hold your breath on the way down," Dorian said.

"What do you mean on the way do—"

Before I could finish my question, the edge of the platform crumbled under my feet. I teetered, waving my arms, trying to rock myself back to stable ground. As my sight panned upwards, I saw Dorian smile.

I fell through misty clouds that broke against my body, my stomach dropping to an unmeasurable depth. The sky was a blue blur that felt never-ending. I braced myself as land rushed up to meet me. I smacked the ground. Pitch black.

My eyes popped open and trapped air burst from my lungs. I was still impaled on a spear but blood was rushing through my veins. My pale skin reddened, its coldness warmed.

I wrapped my hands around the wooden shaft and slowly pulled it from my stomach. The blood was sticky and it was excruciating to feel my insides rip, but I was able to remove the metal head. The wound closed and my skin smoothed, returning to its normal tone. Using my hands, I stretched the skin of my stomach in disbelief.

There wasn't anyone around for miles. The fire had left only remnants of stalls and shoppers. I tried to keep my eyes off the ground, not wanting to accidentally see Hollinshead.

I need to find the necklace. Where did she put it?

I thought back to the night in the shop and the two of us staring out the window. I remembered the look on her face, how surprised and happy she was as I dropped the necklace into her hands.

I walked down an alley that looked like a hurricane had passed through it. The body of the boy who had showed me that spice was on the ground. I stepped carefully along a path created by the corpses of the booksellers.

I needed to jog my memory, so I stopped and closed my eyes. It was so hard to concentrate. All I could think of was drifting through the Nothingness and that feeling of falling.

I opened my eyes. At the end of the alley, Harper's hoodie hung over the dead body of the haggard demon who had told us where to find Moloch. The fire had not reached this row. The hoodie had survived Stolas's onslaught.

My eyes zeroed in on the left pocket as a thought fluttered through my mind, a sudden memory of what Harper had done with the necklace. But it wasn't vivid and I wasn't sure if it was trustworthy.

I jumped onto the table and ripped the hoodie off its hanger. My heart raced as I held it in my hands.

I reached into the left pocket, but it was empty. I closed my eyes, took a deep breath, then slid my hand into the right pocket. My fingers moved around, running along the seam to cover every inch, but again, I was met with disappointment.

I'm screwed.

"Ready?" asked a muffled but familiar voice. I whipped around, and there stood Vlad. He snapped a military salute.

I didn't have the necklace, but I had to keep going. I didn't have a choice. The guy who let Kyle bully him for years would have just given up in Belphegor. I owed it to Harper, but I also owed it to Hollinshead, Moscow, and Thorlton to finish this one way or another.

"Can you take me to Abyzou?" I said.

He nodded and turned to lead me away from the destroyed market and toward the trees. My T-shirt was a mess, so before leaving I changed into a grey one I found.

"How was the fresh-corn picnic?" Vlad said.

"I really didn't have time."

"Okay, but it's a seasonal thing. Just saying."

THE NEEYSON VALLEY

I ran away a lot when I was a kid. Sometimes I'd go to Harper's house, sometimes to Cloaked Atlas, but the odd time I would just wander the Distillery District plying my downtown wiles. This usually got me a few cookies or macarons from a soft-hearted baker or two. The last time I ran away was three years ago, after a fight with my mom. I found her in our backyard and told her that Aaron had punched me in the head. She saw my puffy eyes and told me to deal with it myself, that I wasn't a child anymore. I left. An hour later I was cataloguing some African art for my uncle as he tried to explain the stress of motherhood by telling me the story of Abyzou.

As the demon of motherhood, there was nothing that Abyzou loved more than her daughters. When she refused to call Stolas her ruler, he slaughtered all but one of her daughters, and Abyzou fell into a deep sleep. Her one remaining daughter offered rewards to those who would bring new daughters, in the hopes that enough of them would wake her mother.

Vlad's cape swooshed above our heads as he escorted me through the Neeyson Valley, a blighted hectare of rough, untilled land. This valley had once been home to the young Stolas. It was in these low country fields that he learned the power of the whip and the currency of slaves. It was here that he grew all the hate and disdain that would come to define him.

Vlad was surprisingly chatty. When I asked him why he'd been so quiet when we first met, he said it was to give tourists the full experience. I admired his commitment. He told me all about his role as an escort. He asked about my time in the Nothingness, then reeled off stats about how few made it back. "You can't fool Mara's scale," he said.

We arrived at the rim of the valley, where a small rowboat with chipped black paint rocked back and forth in the light waves of the river. Once we were both seated, Vlad gripped the oars and pushed us away from the muddy shore.

A cipher sailed across the sky, its wings flapping as it circled back and descended toward us. The tip of one wing looked cut off, like the wing of the cipher that cowered in the corner of Stolas's dining room. I had been spotted.

The air smelled of river life. Vlad's effort propelled the boat through the swampy water, past small islands that dotted the way. He carefully navigated through the maze of white tree trunks that broke the glassy plane. I looked back, squinting at the riverbank, now very far away. It felt like I was leaving one world and paddling toward a new one, without Banshees and falling cities and territory patrolled by sharp-toothed Wanderers. It was a false sense of safety, but I appreciated a moment to breathe and not think about the places I'd been, the ones that had scarred me, where those I loved had to stay forever.

Vlad stopped rowing and waited for the boat to ease into shore. When it finally did, I got out. Vlad switched seats so he could paddle back the way we'd come.

"Over the next two hills and through the sycamores, you will find Abyzou's castle," he said, pointing into the forest.

I thanked Vlad and headed away from the shore.

Grabbing on to bendy plant stems to steady myself, I made my way up a steep hill. A strong breeze whistled through the leaves and branches. I realized that this was the first time since Mara that I'd been truly alone.

Another realization hit me: Moloch took Harper from me, her physical body, but Stolas was just as much to blame. He had nailed shut the door that led back to the only home I wanted to return to. The one with my best friend. Maybe I was plagued by blind ambition just like he was. Maybe we were more similar than I wanted to admit.

At Irekeep, Stolas accused me of running from something. He was right. It had been easy to leave home because the idea of a life without Harper was too much to bear. I was running from a future I didn't want. I couldn't just let go.

I recited my plan in my head, as if that would make it any easier to accomplish. *Find Harper, kill Stolas, go home*. There were holes in it. Even if I found Harper, I still had to kill Stolas. If I could kill Stolas, I still had to find a way home. I sucked at plans.

I did have one small advantage. I knew what made Stolas tick. After escaping him the first time, I should have anticipated that he would come after me. This time, though, I was certain I would see him again. He wanted Berdym and slaves. He wanted power, the kind that overthrew emperors and commanded armies. He and Abyzou were longstanding enemies, and there was at least one truth to *The Book of Stolas*: he always went after his enemies. He didn't forgive. He didn't let go.

I reached the grove of sycamores packed tight like sardines. As I got closer to the end of the forest, I could see Abyzou's magnificent castle.

I was surveying the massive land from under a tree when a hooded figure dropped out of the branches, forcing me to the ground. I was flipped onto my back. A face emerged from the cover of a dark hood. The figure threw the hood off her head and we exchanged looks of confused excitement.

I wanted to say, "I missed you and I've thought about you every second since I last saw you." But all that came out was a meek "Hey, buddy."

"I thought you were dead," Hollinshead said, her confusion replaced by a smile and a soft look. She stood and helped me up.

"I was. Kind of."

There was a long moment of silence before Hollinshead wrapped her arms around my neck, pulling our faces together. Her hot cheek was pressed against mine and that warmth filled my body. This moment made the Nothingness worth it.

"They told me you were dead," I said.

"Who?"

"Moscow, my uncle, Harper."

Her puzzled look made me realize I sounded crazy.

"I'll explain later," I said. "How did you survive?"

"Are you new?" she said, her eyebrows slanted. "After he, um, killed you, I was able to get away and make my way here."

Her words prompted an even more important question.

"So why are you here?"

"For Harper," she said, erasing her smile. Her eyes shifted down and remained there. "I was her last chance. I mean, with you and Thorlton, I was always her *only* chance, but … I don't know, I owed it to you."

I didn't know what to say, and I still couldn't believe she was alive. When I'd been with Moscow at the market, I'd touched her dead body and it felt real. But here she was, her hand on my arm.

"So does this mean Thorlton's alive?" I asked.

She shook her head. "He would have wanted us to finish this, and so would Moscow."

We looked at each other awkwardly. She was blushing. As always with her, there was something going on inside her head. I had no idea what it was — until she clutched my shirt and pulled me in.

She kissed me. It was my first kiss, and no matter how many times I'd imagined it, there was no way to actually prepare myself. The lightness, the warmth, the surrounding quiet. Her hand slid up my back and her tongue moved around my mouth. Maybe it was her first kiss, too, and we'd be forever linked by one moment on top of a hill. It was awesome, except for the horrible feeling of guilt that was building in the pit of my stomach. It hurt as much as the spear.

"You're nothing like him," Hollinshead said as we walked toward the castle.

"Think about it. He died and I died. He came back from the dead and I came back from the dead," I said.

"Listen, you're not Freddy Krueger. I don't care how many times you try to convince me."

We stopped to behold Abyzou's castle. On each side of the stately property were octagonal towers. A high stone bridge ran between them.

We entered the castle through the arched wooden doors into a throne room. Every step echoed throughout the room, which had the humbling vastness of a gothic cathedral. It was all grey brick and uneven cobblestone. High above us was a vaulted ceiling. At the far back, wide steps led to a silver throne.

We stopped at a stone well in the middle of the room. I peered in but couldn't see the bottom.

"Why are you here?" We turned to find a middle-aged woman with matted caramel-coloured hair standing next to the throne steps. A black veil covered her face. Hollinshead grabbed my wrist, clearly indicating to me that she would do the talking.

"We're looking for a girl," Hollinshead said. "One of Moloch's."

"I'm Mina. I will take you to Mother," she said, looking at Hollinshead with affection.

We followed her into a large bedroom and right up to the canopy bed that stood in the middle of the room. Under the white lace covering, an old demon lay in smooth satin sheets. Her wrinkled face looked permanently annoyed. Her hands were crossed at her chest.

"Mother, we have visitors. They're looking for one of your daughters," Mina said.

Mina leaned over and put her ear to her mother's chapped lips. She nodded even though the old woman said nothing. I was pretty sure she was dead.

"What is her name?" Mina asked.

"Harper," I replied.

Mina's face changed. The name had struck a nerve.

With total bewilderment, Hollinshead and I watched the scene unfold. Mina whispered into her mother's ear. I struggled to make out what she was saying.

Mina stood up. "Mother says you may find the one you look for."

We followed her down a long dark corridor that narrowed as we reached the adjoining dining hall. The hall was lit only by oil lanterns and smelled of cabbage. Around a long table sat a dozen young girls and women eating soup, their slurping the only sound. I scanned every face in the room, but there was no Harper. The daughters all looked ragged, with tattered clothes and cloudy eyes that followed Hollinshead around the room, obviously making her feel uncomfortable. I wanted to grieve for these people, saddened to think of all their loved ones who were missing them.

We left and ventured down another drafty corridor, which ended at a wall. At the foot of the wall was a darkened half-circle opening.

"She should be in the catacombs. Only one of you can go," Mina said, pointing into the hole.

Hollinshead stepped forward, but I stopped her with my arm.

"I'll go," I said.

"The last time we did this, it didn't end well."

"I know, but it should be me," I said.

Despite her misgivings, Hollinshead relented and stepped back. I crouched down and crawled into the hole. It was tight and murky. I inched forward with my forearms. Cold water dripped on my back. I could hear giggling and whispering from behind the walls, children's laughter delivered via the acoustics of the tunnel. Chalk drawings adorned the stone walls, mostly stick figures of kids playing and family portraits.

I crawled through hair clips, charms, fingernails, bones, and hair that looked like it had been ripped from the roots. Calling it the catacombs made it sound almost pleasant. Charnel house was more appropriate.

Keep moving. Don't think about where you are.

I crawled through an opening and rose to my feet, a streak of sludge down the middle of my body. I looked up a long shaft and saw the ceiling of the throne room and realized I was at the bottom of that well. Three openings were in front of me and, even though they were dark, I was glad to see they were all big enough for me to walk through.

I was startled when a small, clammy hand grabbed mine. I looked down to see a little girl staring up at me with big blue eyes.

"Are you Sam?"

"Yeah, how did you know?"

"She told me about you."

"Who?" I asked, but she just looked at me. I bent down to meet her eyes.

"What's your name?"

"Rose," she said. "C'mon."

Rose tightly held my hand as we walked down the middle tunnel. Halfway in, she pointed to a doorway at the other end.

"She's in there, but I'm not allowed to go."

She handed me a folded piece of paper.

"Will you give this to Billy Nesbitt? He lives in Schenectady. I had nature class with him and he's probably wondering what happened to me."

"Sure," I said, placing the paper in my pocket.

It was hard listening to her request without feeling heartbroken. She ran off, back in the direction we had come. Once through the doorway, I stopped at a rusty ladder that reached to the top of the tall, humid room.

Feet dangled above me, too many to count. My heart raced as I climbed the ladder, passing through the group of women who hung by big hooks under each arm. The hooks were attached to chains that twisted together and were connected to the ceiling.

I pushed bodies out of my way, trying to be as respectful as possible, but several swung back. A few heads slowly turned toward me. Others barely had the strength to moan.

I reached the ceiling but still couldn't find Harper. I moved some more bodies aside, trying to catch a glimpse of others that were hidden behind them. I climbed halfway down. Frantically, I looked through the crowd of pendulous bodies, and then, out of desperation, I screamed Harper's name, only to hear it echo back.

I couldn't ignore the thought any longer, the one that had been rattling and gnawing at me, hanging over me like a dark cloud ever since Harper had disappeared.

She was dead.

I stepped off the last rung onto the damp floor and left, dejected. I made my way back to the throne room, where Rose was sitting against the well. I crouched beside her.

"She wasn't there," I said.

I was also wondering where Hollinshead was. Something didn't feel right.

"She's gone," Rose said nervously.

"What do you mean? Did something happen to her?"

"She left. Mother made me lie to you. I'm sorry."

Hollinshead's distant voice called my name. I looked all around, confused as to where she was. A feeling of dread was creeping quickly through my nerves.

She yelled my name again, this time more fearfully.

Her voice was coming from outside. I fought my buckling knees and grappled with the anticipation of what was waiting for me there. As I neared the castle door, I stepped over Mina's dead body, troubled by the sight of her blood on the floor and knowing that I was about to walk into danger.

As my feet touched grass, I saw that things had taken a turn for the worse. In the stretch of land between Abyzou's castle and the forest, Hollinshead lay on her stomach. Her hair clung to her sweaty face and dirt covered her cheeks. A line of blood dripped down the side of her head. A sword was pointed at the back of her neck. Stolas held the sword.

This was the last thing I needed right now.

"My cipher didn't lie. He was tracking the girl here but came back with word that you were alive," Stolas said.

He pulled a long horn made of polished bone out of his belt. "This is Adramelech's Horn, and outside of Alchem's Gifts, it might be the most cherished possession in Hell. Doesn't look like much but it helped end the reign of an emperor. Without the Wanderers, the emperor was nothing, too pathetic to achieve conquest on his own."

He placed his lips on the small end and blew as hard as he could. A trumpet-like blast shook the trees. Hollinshead and I covered our ears from the ear-splitting sound.

An acrid and familiar smell wafted through the air. The ground convulsed, sending vibrations through my body. The vibrations kept getting stronger, ending when talons broke through the dirt.

Under the red sky, sinewy bodies bloomed out of the ground. Dirt cascaded off their heads, across their stitched eyelids, and over their lips. They announced their arrival by a rapid series of squeals, each followed by grunts so harsh they could be mistaken for a thunderclap. The land had given birth to an army of Wanderers.

"Oh shit," I said.

Hollinshead, face clenched, was looking to me for answers. I had nothing.

Enemies surrounded me on all sides. I tried to keep a calm exterior, even though my insides were a panicked, gooey mess.

Stolas stood imperially, wearing his arrogance like a crown. "I hate that I'm starting to admire you, Sam," he said. His stare intensified, as did his grip on the horn. "You didn't find your friend. I told you, she belongs to Hell now."

He was right. I was screwed.

Stolas dropped the sword, grabbed me by my hair, and pulled me toward the anxious creatures who were waiting to be released from their imaginary pen. He threw me at their feet and then walked back toward the door of the castle. A salivating Wanderer raked its foot against the ground, waiting for permission to charge.

Another deafening horn blast, then the stampede began. I stumbled around, holding my breath, waiting to be mauled. The Wanderers slid to a stop all around me. One bit into my leg before another dragged me toward the forest by my shirt, wanting me all to itself. Others followed us, snapping and clawing at me. They converged over me like hungry pigs at a trough. They were so precise, it was as if their teeth had eyes.

A spot of blood on my shirt grew into a stain and dark red soaked into my jeans. Two Wanderers chomped on my arm, another narrowly missed my neck, and the rest tried to squeeze their heads in to gnaw at whatever part of me they could reach.

Through the throng of bodies, I could see the castle doors, where Stolas held Hollinshead in place by her arms. She had the same expression on her face as the last time she'd watched me die. Her lips moved to scream, but I couldn't hear her over the growling and grunting.

The Wanderers paused to fight among themselves, circling and snapping their frightful maws. Their hot breath whistled through their noses. Their divided attention gave me just enough time to crawl closer to the forest, even though I'd conceded there was nowhere to go.

A Wanderer jumped on my back, shoving me hard onto the ground. I spat up more blood. Another stepped on the cuts on my arm, making me cry out in pain.

I am ready to die.

They stepped back and joined the others who were standing around me snarling, saliva dripping from their mouths. I pulled myself to my knees. I breathed heavily, phlegm and dirt clogging my lungs. Harper floated through my mind. Wherever she was, I hoped she was safe.

A vicious claw slashed my back, and I screamed from the searing pain as I fell forward.

I can't do this anymore.

Close by, something was rolling toward me, cracking dry nettles and leaves. A Wanderer's talons scraped my back, this time in the opposite direction than the last.

Between two trees, a yawning metal tube poked out, almost touching my face. It was a cannon, and there was a definite sizzling sound coming from it. Hidden by shadows, a figure from atop the cannon said, "Sam. Sam. Down." The figure jumped off, revealing a spark eating its way down a fuse.

"Huh?" I said, raising an eyebrow, trying to understand what was happening. Was this a hallucination, the effect of blood loss?

Barely any of the fuse remained. I dropped to my stomach and covered my head with my hands as the spark devoured the rest of the fuse and entered the cannon. My anticipation mounted as the area quieted for a moment that felt like an hour.

The cannon jerked back and then, as it cocked forward, a black cannonball exploded out of a cloud of grey smoke. A burst of hot air screeched over my backside. The ball smashed into the surprised herd of Wanderers, crushing their bones and mashing their faces until it eventually landed and rolled toward the entrance of the castle.

Again, the land grew quiet. The smell of gunpowder floated above us. I looked behind me and saw the blood-stained skin and bashed skulls of several Wanderers.

The sound of hundreds of twigs cracking filled the forest as more shadowy figures scurried through the trees. Only a few feet from where I lay, a Wanderer ran to the edge of the forest and sniffed the hole of the cannon. It stepped to the side, and as soon it did, the back of its head burst open and a sharp metal point appeared out of its skull.

The remaining Wanderers — there were still dozens — arched their backs and stiffly turned toward the forest, where the sound of crunching leaves got louder and louder. Suddenly, the forest released a horde of armoured Incubi and Succubi, brandishing swords, spears, and maces. Their bodies flashed past me.

Before I could get up, a Wanderer lunged at me. We barrel rolled, ending with it on top, its talons pushing down my shoulder. I grabbed its head, which was just a thin layer of skin over a bony skull. I fought to hold it back, trying to keep its hands away from my jugular. I dug my thumbs into its closed eyes, ripping part of the stitching. It pushed forward against my thumbs. Just before the Wanderer could bite into my face, a blade was jammed into its back. It toppled over. Behind the fresh corpse stood Thorlton, covered in blood. Happiness momentarily replaced my pain.

"Sam! Sam!" he said as he leaped into my arms. I was running on fumes at that point. All I could do was close my eyes and pass out.

21
EVERYONE FROM EVERYWHERE

This memory was my favourite. Harper and I were seven years old and lying on sleeping bags in my dark bedroom. Flashlights in hand, we battled our circles of light on the ceiling, the fate of the Rebel Alliance hanging in the balance. As our arms got tired, our circles stopped swirling. They slowly moved closer together until they slightly overlapped.

"They're kissing, Sam." Harper gave a high-pitched laugh. We held the beams of light in place.

My mind shifted to the market. I was standing with Hollinshead. Our eyes locked as I brushed back her hair to reveal her shy smile.

The memories mingled, each indistinguishable from the other.

Am I in the Nothingness again? Am I dead?

I heard both of their voices, Harper's calling my name and Hollinshead's aggressively trying to coax me awake.

Am I dreaming?

Violent screaming. The clanking of metal. A powerful flap of wings. The hard squish of cut tissue. More screaming.

My eyes slivered open. Harsh daylight blotted out the blurry images in front of me. The red sky seemed a thousand miles away, but hovering right over me were two familiar faces: Harper and Hollinshead.

Yup, I'm dead. Crap.

"Finally," Hollinshead said.

"Sam!" Harper wrapped her arms around my neck and buried her head into my chest. I put my arm around her. She was warm. She was real.

What's happening?

"Sam! Sam! Sam!" Thorlton broke between the two of them and gave me a chokehold of a hug. I was starting to remember what had happened before I passed out: the Wanderers, the cannon, Stolas.

I sat up and there was Harper sitting right next to me, wiping away tears. I was speechless thinking about how Moscow had been right; just seeing her made me feel as though I were home again. She was nothing like the Harper I'd encountered in the Black Arch Forest or in the Nothingness. Sure, she was thinner and bruised, her hair ratty, but this was the real Harper and she didn't belong to Hell. I should have known. Harper would never just sit around waiting to be rescued. The person from my memory finally merged with the person before me, creating the real Harper. The anti–Princess Buttercup.

"You came for me," she said, her voice so gleeful it could have belonged to a choir of angels. She gave me another hug. I was choked by tears.

"Of course I did," I said. "Where have you been?"

She told me how she had escaped Mina and by chance had found Dashiell, who she remembered from the book I had shown her when we were in the private collection room. He convinced a family to hide her. When he came back to check on her, he told her about everything that had happened between Stolas and me and that he was on his way to the Demon Mother's castle and impending battle. She begged him to take her with him. When they arrived, Hollinshead was pulling my body up this hill.

Hollinshead walked away and mounted a horse that had been left tied to a nearby tree. She was staring straight ahead, distraught about something.

I slowly got up and tried to get my bearings. The sounds I'd heard while unconscious weren't the soundtrack to a dream. I had passed out during a fight only to awake in a battle, one that would finally lay to rest the Hell I'd loved as a kid and reveal the true nature of this world. From our vantage on the hill, we could see a storm of commotion on the field below us. It was chaos: fast and loud, wild and vicious. In front of Abyzou's castle was a bleak, tangled mess of angry faces, dirty bodies, bared teeth, and corpses. Krauss, Arkavelle, and Volac soldiers, along with a platoon of Incubi and Succubi, battled an army of Stolas supporters made up of Hanbi demons and Alpsecords, joined by the few remaining Wanderers. Both sides had an identical mission: mash, slice, cut limbs from bodies, swing a weapon, pull it back covered in your enemy's blood, turn before the same happened to you. Stolas watched from the top of another hill.

The Volacs soared on winged serpents, laying siege to vultures and averting the rain of arrows flying from the bows of the Alpsecords below them. The Hanbi avoided the blades of the advancing Arkavelles. When they could, the Hanbi struck with their teeth, aiming for throats and faces. The Krauss, many with half-severed wings, stood back to back, trying to fend off the last of the Wanderers. In the distance, an armoured demon with the head of a wolf led the Incubi and Succubi through the field toward Stolas. I would later learn that this was Dashiell. He had protected Harper.

Ciphers sat in the trees, waiting to carry word of victory to every town and city. Banshees were perched on the roof of the castle, their eyes glued on Stolas. They wanted their bones back.

I rubbed my face, trying to understand how all of this had happened, how everything had turned on me. I walked over to Hollinshead and placed my hand on top of her hand. "We need to get out of here," I said.

"We made a pact. If Stolas survives, then we're screwed," she replied.

There was so much going on that I had forgotten about the pact with Gary, another one of my mistakes.

"Then take Harper and Thorlton and leave. Find another way home. I'll stay," I said.

She removed her hand from under mine and gripped the pommel of the saddle, looking despondent, her eyebrows knit. Her face carried the weight of our entire time together and the burden I had placed on her.

"And then what? Trusting the next Pazuzu to help me and being responsible for Harper as well?" she said.

"Or if I do find a way home, wondering if red fog is behind every door?"

She took a deep, unsure breath, her eyes filled with pain. "This is my life, Sam," she said. "I was never meant to go home."

"I don't believe that," I said. "Listen to me —"

"You got your *friend* back. That's what you wanted all along, right?" she said, her eyes downcast. "Doesn't matter what happens to me."

"Yes, it does."

Harper got up and stood beside me. She had been listening, but looked lost. She and Hollinshead shared a long, thoughtful look. It felt like each wanted to question the other's intentions.

"He's a good one," Hollinshead said, pointing at me. "He's very brave."

She gave a coy wink, then turned and galloped toward the action. It was a pathetic goodbye cut short by a greater calling. As many tried to escape the bloodshed, Hollinshead marched right into the thick of it.

I held Harper's hand as we watched Hollinshead together. There was only one emotion swirling inside of me. I was scared. Scared of dying, scared that Hollinshead would be killed, scared of something bad happening to Thorlton, scared that Harper would be stuck in this world. Scared of failing.

Hidden somewhere in the adrenalin rush of fear was a whisper of courage. I turned to Harper and kissed her. It was long and sloppy and perfect. I had waited my whole life for this, and every second of our first kiss was better than I had imagined it would be. I placed my hands on either side of her face and we held our lips together for a long moment. My mouth felt paralyzed. My brain fired off every feeling it knew. For the first time in a long time, I felt free.

But I had to pull away.

"I can't let her do this alone," I said, our foreheads touching.

"It's too dangerous," Harper replied.

"But this is all my fault."

"I want to show you something," she said.

Harper pulled something out of her pocket. She held her fist dramatically above our heads. When she opened her hand, out dropped the necklace, dangling from her index finger. I couldn't believe my eyes.

"You're kidding," I said.

She handed it to me. I was overwhelmed with so much emotion that for a moment I even forgot to be scared.

"I stole it from a goat lady at some market," Harper said. "Bitch had my hoodie."

"So you know what it is?"

"What are you talking about?" She bit her lip. "I wanted it back. It was the only thing I had to remember you by."

I caressed her face before looking out over the battlefield, where Hollinshead's horse weaved through the violence. Holding on to the pommel, she dropped over the side of the horse, almost parallel to the ground, and pulled a sword out of the stomach of an Alpsecord as she rode by.

I explained my theory about the necklace to Harper. But there was a hitch. The necklace had no inscription.

I studied every link of the chain, trying to find a word or sentence that could bring the red fog. But there was nothing.

Thorlton ran up to us, fear in his eyes. "Have to help!" he said. He hugged my leg, then headed toward the fighting.

A cipher flew overhead. An idea struck me. I called to Thorlton.

"Get a cipher!" I said, pointing to the trees where they were waiting.

He nodded and ran off. My eyes stayed on Hollinshead, following her as she tried to fight her way to Stolas.

Moments later, a cipher landed at our feet. Thorlton ran behind him to rejoin me. I gave the cipher the necklace and my instructions. He shot me a curious look, then flew across the battlefield.

"Now what?" Harper said.

"We hope that Stolas knows what to do and that I didn't just do something really stupid," I said. I didn't mention the pact to her. I was still working that part out.

Thorlton started to run toward the battle again.

"Stay here," I said to him.

He seemed confused, but I wasn't in the mood to explain myself. I just wanted to keep everyone I cared about safe for as long as I could.

Far away, Hollinshead ripped her sword out of the shoulder of a Hanbi. She was much closer to Stolas now, who was still watching from the top of his hill, but she was too late. I had sabotaged her plan — well, that is, if my plan worked.

The cipher flew to Stolas and dropped the necklace into his hand. Stolas looked in our direction, a terrible grin spreading across his face. Out of nowhere a wave of red light swept over the field, catching the attention of every warrior. The fighting ceased as everyone turned to look for its source. A few immediately fled.

Stolas turned away from us. His spine broke through the skin of his arched back. He released a harrowing scream as two enormous wings of blade-like feathers emerged from his body. Everyone on the field cowered as Stolas transformed into Alchem.

Silently, we all watched him march down the hill to the centre of the field. The Hanbi respectfully bowed in his presence. He seemed to take note of those who didn't. Sensing what would come next, the remaining Krauss flew away. The Incubi and Succubi were shaken but refused to surrender their weapons.

The box had been a door, but with the necklace, I didn't know where the fog would appear. From the hilltop, I scanned the area, increasingly desperate, my eyes seeking strands of fog in the mayhem. Finally, I saw it. Red fog seeped out from under the door of Abyzou's castle, spreading along the ground in front. I could barely contain my excitement. I grabbed Harper's arm and pointed at the castle. At least part of my plan had worked.

Our sweet moment was shattered when the fighting resumed, this time even fiercer, with Stolas both the target and the aggressor. He was a force, fighting the charging hordes with little effort.

A terrified Harper and I ran through the forest, trying to close the ground between us and Hollinshead and between us and the fog. It was easy to go undetected, since everyone was paying attention to Stolas.

Hollinshead stood in attack position behind the cover of some Volacs, whose serpents had been killed. Her face was covered in dirt and blood, a large gash on her arm. I snuck across the field, making my way to her, and whipped her around. A very bad idea, since she almost stabbed me.

"What are you doing here?" she said. "You need to leave."

"We need your help getting to the castle."

She looked over and saw what was happening at the door.

"Where's Harper?" Hollinshead said.

"Hiding in the forest."

"Let's go get her."

We found Harper at the edge of the forest, reluctant to leave the safe shelter provided by the trees. She was crouched behind a thick trunk and seemed overwhelmed by the violence.

"Once we start running, don't stop," Hollinshead said.

Harper didn't care for the command. "Why are we listening to her?"

"We don't have time to argue. Just trust her," I said. Judging by the look on Hollinshead's face, she appreciated what I had said.

Between the red fog and us was a field choked with battle. We ran hard through a path of soldiers either dead or crying for help. I could feel the cold eyes of the Banshees watching us from above.

Hollinshead kept urging us on with shouts of "Go! Go!" When I stopped hearing her voice, I knew something was wrong. I slid to a stop and turned to see that she had tripped over a Hanbi whose face was smeared with blood. He stood, knocked the sword out of her hand, and pushed her to the ground.

"Keep going!" I shouted to Harper. I ran back and threw myself into the Hanbi's midsection before he could strike Hollinshead with his teeth. We landed on the ground close to Hollinshead's sword. She was crawling toward it, but I picked it up before she could reach it. As the Hanbi turned to attack me, I shoved it into his shoulder. He screamed and darted away.

Hollinshead helped me up and I handed her her sword. We pounded across the field to catch up with Harper. I held my breath, waiting for an arrow to hit me in the back. Fog began to cover our feet. We were at the door to the castle.

Hollinshead stood guard as I tugged on the heavy door. As I pulled it open, sunlight crossed the threshold into Hell.

The door was now fully opened, red fog crawling up the surrounding stone. I closed my eyes and briefly enjoyed the comforting breeze that carried the low heat of the sun. My sun. I opened my eyes and saw before me a golden field under a light-blue sky. My sky. Far off, a truck drove down a strip of road. It could have been a rotting landfill and it wouldn't have mattered. It was home.

My focus returned.

"Harper," I said. I dug Rose's note to Billy Nesbitt out of my pocket. "Take this. I'll explain later."

She took the note, barely able to pry her eyes from the scene on the other side of the door.

"You go first," I said.

She ran through the door. Once on the other side, she broke down in tears.

Hollinshead dropped her sword to her side as she solemnly looked at the world she hadn't seen since she was a child. Her eyes watered. We looked at each other for a second or two before she hugged me for the last time. I thought of all she had done for me.

"Not bad, Sam," she whispered into my ear.

We turned to look through the door once more. I moved behind her, hoping it wouldn't arouse her suspicion. There was no chance I was going to leave her — she just didn't know it yet.

I'm not exactly proud of what I did next, but let's be honest: Hollinshead was stronger than I was and a thousand times more stubborn. She would eventually forgive me, I thought, or at least I hoped so.

Threads of the red fog crept toward Hollinshead, but she didn't notice, her gaze through the door unbroken. The thin wisps collected, and like the first time, they formed hands that clutched Hollinshead's legs and arms. A quick pull alerted her to what was happening, but it was too late. I grabbed the sword from her hand and pushed her forward. She turned, struggling to get back.

"No!" she yelled.

She fell, her fingernails scraping the stone, but the fog was too powerful. It pulled her through the door and back to where she belonged.

Harper sprinted toward me. I closed the door, cutting off the sound of the two of them screaming my name. I pressed my shoulder to the wood and waited for the fog to disappear.

It was over.

I was gut-wrenchingly alone, or as alone as I could be considering I was surrounded by a horde of demons on a busy battlefield. I felt like someone had reached into my chest and squeezed my heart until it popped. I touched the warm door, knowing that on the other side there was once more just a well in an empty room.

All my fear settled into the pit of my stomach like gravel in a stream, but I didn't have the luxury of just standing around. With Hollinshead's sword in my hand, I walked to a horse that was tied to a tree near the castle entrance.

Time to take stock of my situation: I had a horse, a sword, and the burden of killing the biggest demon on the battlefield, the one who was thinning the crowd as if it were child's play.

I gripped the reins. I'd be lying if I said my first thought wasn't to ride in the opposite direction. But I couldn't bring myself to turn the horse around. There was no one left to deal with my mistake. No, it was on me to finish this.

Stolas was tearing a violent swath through the field, making his way to Dashiell. With all his might, Dashiell swung his sword, but Stolas ducked away from its trajectory. Dashiell swung several more times, but each time his blade seemed to just bounce off Stolas's shoulders, neck, or leg. Dashiell regrouped, and with two hands on his sword, he swung with every ounce of his frustration. His strike missed Stolas's midsection but the tip left a long, bloody cut. A vulnerability.

I took off toward them, moving with the chaos. Every bit of distance I closed between us made my situation that more real.

As I got closer, Stolas turned and saw me. There was determination in his eyes. He readied himself to charge, but as he started to run, the Banshees swarmed him. They clutched his arms and shoulders, trying to pull him into the air. He shook them loose, stomping on one who fell on her side.

My head was spinning. All my thoughts fired at once: Dorian's warning. The weight of the sword in my hand. The gritty feel of the handle. Hooves trampling the ground and bodies, kicking up dirt. I gripped my sword tightly and raised it high. *No*, I thought, *I need to loosen my grip*, remembering how my uncle had taught me to squeeze just before connecting. "Like a punch," he would say.

I had never punched anyone, not even Kyle. I had died, though. I had kept going. Maybe it did just take me a little longer to mature, or maybe people were wrong about me.

I was thundering toward Stolas, seconds away from him, when everything slowed. I took the deepest breath I had ever taken.

One decisive strike.

Without hesitation, I thrust the sword forward. My strike was so hard, so clean, that it slid right through Stolas's skin and into his stomach. He screamed and writhed, scaring my horse, which reared back, twisted, and then fell onto its side, throwing me to the hard ground.

Stolas fell to his knees. He slumped, his head bobbing. The wings dissolved to bone, then the bones broke apart into powdery dust. He was once again the demon I sailed along the River Styx with, the one that had betrayed me at Irekeep.

Dashiell plunged his sword into Stolas's neck, and then swiftly pulled it out, releasing the blood like a burst pipe. Stolas keeled forward, which pushed my sword even deeper inside of him.

The Banshees formed a circle around Stolas. They started rocking back and forth and whispering in unison. Stolas's skin melted into the ground, leaving just his bones. Still whispering, the Banshees flew off in the direction of Belphegor. The bones followed them. I watched until they were only dots in the distance.

The Hanbi and Alpsecords retreated. The ciphers shot out of the trees to spread the word throughout Hell. The sky rained ash.

Covered in dirt and blood, I lay on my back and oriented myself with the red sky. Despite everything, there was no denying how I was feeling. Happy.

The field was deathly quiet. There was a sense of shock, both for the victory and because it was all over.

"Sam, Sam, Sam." Thorlton ran over to help me up.

I stood before the watchful gaze of the crowd. I honestly didn't know who was on my side and who was thinking about killing me. There were so many eyes on me.

Dashiell dropped to one knee. Then another demon followed. Slowly, each demon, no matter how injured or aching, kneeled before me.

The Defeater of Stolas.

All right, I'd have to work on the name.

SAM SULLINGER

efore leaving, Thorlton and I searched the entire field for the necklace, but we found only a few broken links, which I collected in my pocket. Dashiell told me that it had most likely been destroyed along with its holder. *Nice work, Sam*, I thought.

It felt strange when we finally left the battlefield. When it's over, you kind of just walk away, changed and grateful. The horror doesn't sink in for some time. I tried not to look back, but when my horse reached the top of the hill, I couldn't resist. The scene was like a mural painted with dirt clumps and languishing bodies.

I rode with Dashiell along the same river that had brought me to the Neeyson Valley. Thorlton sat in front of me, happily bopping with each trot. I think he understood my decision.

Thorlton explained what had happened at the colony. A cipher had arrived hours before Stolas. Most of the Incubi and Succubi moved deeper into the woods.

Gary and a few who stayed behind were killed, but Ruthie was safe and waiting for Thorlton.

I asked him why he had come to Abyzou's, and his answer was simple and Thorlton-like. All he said was "Sam. Sam."

As we rode, I once again found myself missing Harper. The whole point of my journey had been to rid myself of that horrible feeling, to expel that emptiness. It was worse now, but I'd have to just accept it.

I also missed Hollinshead, and I couldn't lie to myself anymore. I was in love with her. As my friend Moscow would have said, she had become my new home, someone who kept my head above the rocky water on my journey. My feelings ricocheted between the two of them. There was no way to reconcile how I felt. All I could do was hope that I would see them again.

Then there was my family, even my dad. I wished they could meet the new me, the last soldier to leave the battlefield. I'd miss them, but nothing compared to how I would miss Uncle Bear. Maybe he, Raymond, and Hollinshead would share a bottle of W.L. Weller in my honour. That thought warmed me.

My horse caught up to Dashiell. He had offered me a place to stay in his lighthouse in Ep Sumter. From there, I had no plan. But hey, Hell was a big world. I'd figure something out.

I always do.

EPILOGUE

S hadows danced across the leather-bound books. The shelves and display cases were caked in a layer of dust, every trinket speckled. On the wall of swords, two hooks were empty. The back of the shop, once a hidden treasure trove, was now cleared out, the private collection that reflected a lifetime of work relegated to a basement corner in a building on the University of Toronto campus.

Cloaked Atlas was dark and lifeless, all of its quirky clientele turned away at the door by a disinterested shop owner. There was talk of closing it down. Without Sam, everything felt empty and pointless.

Photos of Sam and Harper were plastered all over the news. The narrative was made digestible: a bullied kid and an overachieving student were missing. Two kids on the run, one from pain and the other from pressure. They were the focus of a press conference and a search party, and their teachers and peers were interrogated. No one could find the smallest trace of them.

Sam's dad, Glen, had been coming by the shop every day. He and Bear would sit in the back office as Glen, eyes puffy and face stubbly, poured out regrets and asked a hundred questions about his son. Spliced between the questions were memories of Sam. At first, Bear thought Glen was accusing him of having something to do with Sam's disappearance. But as the conversations progressed, it became clear that he was only trying to unravel the mystery of the young man who lived under his roof but had drifted so far away.

Glen once asked if Sam ever spoke about him. He wanted to know if Sam felt loved even though that word was never spoken. Bear lied to his brother-in-law, reassuring him that his son knew that he had a happy home and a caring father.

Bear sat in the reading nook, his hand on his chin as he stared at the cold fireplace. The ashes of *The Book of Stolas* were indistinguishable from those of logs and old newspapers. He ran his other hand over Sam's sword, which was resting on his lap. He couldn't stop his brain from mining the past.

He remembered why he'd annexed this small corner of his shop as a reading nook for his nephew. It was to get him to stop rummaging around so much, poking around dangerous things. He also thought it would be nice for Sam to be surrounded by stories of adventure and romance, words that could guide him through all of the problems he was having at home and at school. Bear used to tell Raymond that it would take only one story to right the boy's ship.

Bear took a deep breath that ended with a phlegmy cough. He turned his wheelchair around to leave the room, but was stunned by a familiar face in the dark doorway.

"Hi," the figure struggled to say.

He wheeled forward, needing the moonlight to capture her face and confirm her identity. She looked weary and on the verge of tears as she bent down to hug him.

"Harper," Bear said, struggling under the weight of uncertainty. He felt like he did in the few seconds before he fell asleep, reality drifting into a dream state. He stroked her face. It was warm. "I can't believe it's you."

His tears soaked the shoulder of her shirt as he fired off a series of thank yous to God, the universe, Zeus, whoever was listening. Harper pulled back as another figure stepped from the stairwell and hovered in the doorway.

Bear squinted and said, "Sam."

"This is Sam's friend," Harper said. "She helped him."

The young woman stepped out of the darkness, an immense sadness burdening her face. Bear looked at her softly. They exchanged painful smiles, tormented by the same thought.

"Where is he?" Bear asked, refusing to let go of Harper's hand. She was squeezing his just as tight.

"He didn't come back." Harper said.

"Please tell me he's still alive."

Harper dropped her head and didn't answer.

"We don't know," Hollinshead said. "But he does have a way of not dying."

Hollinshead walked to the middle of the shop. She saw photos of Sam taped to the cash register and a shelf lined with The Books of Hell. She felt as if she were once again in the presence of her friend.

"He saved us," Hollinshead said, shaking her head with disbelief. She looked at Bear. "He's a hero."

Bear smiled. He smiled for his nephew, who was more like a son, because he had accomplished something exceptional, something no one could ever take away from him. A legacy of sorts.

He also smiled because a plan was taking shape in his cagey, clever old brain.

ACKNOWLEDGEMENTS

Writing a novel is a solitary experience, yet there are still a lot of people who helped and encouraged me along the way.

I am deeply grateful to the entire team at Dundurn, not only for their efforts but for their belief in the novel. In particular, Rachel Spence for acquiring the novel, along with Scott Fraser, Jenny McWha, Laura Boyle, Sophie Paas-Lang, Sara D'Agostino, Stephanie Ellis, Elena Radic, and Elham Ali. Thank you to my editor, Susan Fitzgerald, for catching my mistakes (there were a few) but more so for truly understanding the story I was trying to tell.

A big thank you to Joseph Kertes for his time, insights, and support from the very beginning and for his mentorship throughout the writing process, and then for navigating me through the publishing world.

For their constant support, I would like to thank Jason and Michelle Shapiro. My mom, Marian Shapiro, who bought books for me without question and let me watch whatever movies and TV shows I wanted. While many were questionable, they undoubtedly nurtured my love of stories. I am also grateful to Helen Kertes, Angela Kertes, Jordan Sugar, Lorne Frohman, Barbara Berson, and Ty Templeton. And to my nieces and nephews, Ella Shapiro, Chase Shapiro (who loves reading), Dylan Sugar, and Sadie Sugar. Thank you to friends who read early drafts of my work or listen to me talk about them: Nick Wakeham, Josh Saltzman, Jamila-Khanom Allidina and Mark LeRoy.

The Wattpad community read the first two (very rough) drafts of my novel. Their engagement with the world and characters spurred me on. To anyone who clicked the star, shared it, left a comment or reached out directly — thank you. It's hard to put a story out into the world; it's something truly personal. The response from those early Wattpad readers meant a lot.

This book would only be a glorious Word document if not for my wife, Natalie. Her support, honesty and ability to corral both me and my imagination, which I've learned can be a challenge (magic hands), is invaluable. You sat through countless breakfast brainstorms, were my first editor, helped me write hundreds of queries, and steered me in the right direction, which wasn't always clear. Most importantly, you were right.

Thanks to Sydney, my baby daughter, my good luck charm. No rush, but when you get around to reading my story, I hope you like it even though it has no pop-out bunnies or owls that go "whoo."

CPSIA information can be obtained
at www.ICGtesting.com
Printed in the USA
LVHW052007240820
664081LV00008B/1193

9 781459 746756